Chinaberry

James Still

CHINABERRY

EDITED BY SILAS HOUSE

THE UNIVERSITY PRESS of KENTUCKY

THE UNIVERSITY PRESS OF KENTUCKY

Scholarly publisher for the Commonwealth, serving Bellarmine University, Berea College, Centre College of Kentucky, Eastern Kentucky University, The Filson Historical Society, Georgetown College, Kentucky Historical Society, Kentucky State University, Morehead State University, Murray State University, Northern Kentucky University, Transylvania University, University of Kentucky, University of Louisville, and Western Kentucky University. All rights reserved.

Editorial and Sales Offices: The University Press of Kentucky
663 South Limestone Street, Lexington, Kentucky 40508-4008

www.kentuckypress.com

15 14 13 12 11   5 4 3 2 1

Frontispiece: James Still, ca. 1990. Courtesy of Teresa Reynolds.

Library of Congress Cataloging-in-Publication Data

Still, James, 1906-2001.
Chinaberry / James Still ; edited by Silas House.
p. cm.
ISBN 978-0-8131-3372-0 (hardcover : acid-free paper) —
ISBN 978-0-8131-3373-7 (ebook)
I. House, Silas, 1971- II. Title.
PS3537.T5377C47   2011
813'.52—DC22

2010054018

This book is printed on acid-free recycled paper meeting the requirements of the American National Standard for Permanence in Paper for Printed Library Materials.

Manufactured in the United States of America.

Member of the Association of American University Presses

BOOK DESIGN *by* VIN DANG

Childhood is less clear to me than to many people: when it ended I turned my face away from it for no reason I know about. . . . Then I discovered that the tales of former children are seldom to be trusted. Some people supply too many past victories or pleasures with which to comfort themselves, and other people cling to pains, real and imagined, to excuse what they have become.

LILLIAN HELLMAN, *Pentimento*

Here was a reality more powerful than the present.

JAMES STILL, found among his notes on this manuscript

CONTENTS

Silas House

WHEN JAMES STILL'S literary advisers, Bill Marshall, Lee Smith, and Bill Weinberg, first asked me, back in 2004, if I would be interested in editing the manuscript James Still had left behind at his death, I didn't even have to think twice. I agreed instantly, feeling daunted but also incredibly blessed to have an opportunity to work on a manuscript by one of my literary heroes.

For the uninitiated, a brief primer on that hero: James Still, born in 1906, is widely considered "the Dean of Appalachian Literature." He is the author of such classics as *River of Earth* (1940) and *The Wolfpen Poems* (1986). He was an accomplished stylist known for his keen insights into the nature of people, animals, and the living, breathing world around him, a man who swooned for words and for trees. His novels and short stories and poetry are at the very heart of Appalachian literature. A native of Alabama, he came to Kentucky to work for the Hindman Settlement School in 1932 and never left, living there until his death at ninety-four years old.

Mr. Still is also someone I knew from a distance. As an aspiring writer attending the Appalachian Writers Workshop at Hindman, I crept about the edges of his conversation, too in awe to ever have a real exchange. Sixty-five years his junior, I had been raised on his books, had grown up knowing him as the great writer who lived only three counties away from me. I once had my picture taken with him but was too awestruck to speak. The one time we actually talked, a year later, I asked him how to become a better writer. He told me to "discover something new every day." This simple advice changed my writing and my life, making me more aware of every single thing as I walked through each day. I do not claim to have been his friend; it is enough to have been in his presence.

I couldn't wait to get started on the manuscript, but life kept interfering. Two years after accepting the challenge to edit the manuscript, Lee Smith presented me with Mr. Still's briefcase—he had fashioned an old belt to stand in for its broken handle—and having that helped to center me and gave me the proper kick to get started. At last I was able to sit down and completely immerse myself in the book that has now changed me forever by showing me that every single sentence in any book has to be fretted over, polished, pruned, and also by solidifying my notion that the best writing has to be packed tight with emotion. Over the next three months I trekked down to my little writer's shack every morning, fired up about helping to bring forth what I have come to think of as the book that Mr. Still most wanted to write. I think of it that way because I believe there is a yearning woven into every line, a longing to share his hard-won wisdom with as many readers as possible. Four more years have swept past us all since I finished the edit of the book.

The story of a young, unnamed boy who travels to Texas without his parents and is taken in by a grieving rancher and his beautiful wife, *Chinaberry* is a remarkable capturing of a place and time that is gone forever, a place of ranches that went on for miles and miles, of cotton fields that stretched to the horizon, of free-range cattle, and of schools that were set up by the ranchers themselves. This is a book that forever preserves a place and time in history that might have been forgotten otherwise. And while it is a beautiful look at a pivotal time in the narrator's childhood, it is also an unforgettable portrait of the people that narrator came to know during this trip to Texas: sad, troubled, yet confident Anson Winters; his caring and tender wife, Lurie; Ernest Roughton, the narrator's honest and solid caretaker; the Knuckleheads, two inseparable friends who enjoy nothing more than a good prank (and are obviously literary kin to Harl and Tibb Logan, the prankster cousins in *River of Earth*).

In editing this book, my main goal was to stay completely true to Mr. Still's intentions in creating plot, theme, tone, and syntax. His precise, elegant language and wonderful rhythm— each sentence taut with a specific beat that you can almost tap your foot to—were present throughout the original manuscript, even though he didn't complete the book before his death.

For the most part, the manuscript was in excellent shape. Some chapters are presented here just as he wrote them, with almost no changes. His ability to write a tight, lyrical sentence on the first try is absolutely amazing, and this is some of his finest prose. Witness this line, picked at random: "We had arrived at siesta, that period between high noon and two when the Texas sun is at its most torrid and brightest, and the leaves of the trees hang limp and blades of the corn curl." Within this sentence lies an entire world, and it is a sentence wrought with action, imagery, and the senses. Note how perfectly the monosyllabic words are spaced out from the polysyllabic words, the strength of this sentence's construction. A reader could sing this line aloud if she took a notion and all the while feel the heat of the Texas sun on her neck, smell the corn baking in the fields, and see the limp leaves on the trees. A whole way of life packed into one rhythmic and lovely sentence. This book sings with the strength of a writer working at the height of his powers.

Occasionally the chapters were too short or episodic, and it seemed obvious that these were instances in which Mr. Still was just laying down notes so he could polish them up and stretch them out when he could turn his attention back to the book. In these instances I usually combined chapters or scenes, adding only brief transitional sentences to keep the flow from being interrupted and to preserve the beautiful rhythm that he had established so well. Only occasionally did I add a few words or a sentence. And sometimes I had to hope I was choosing correctly without any real direction from Mr. Still. For example, in the original manuscript, Ernest is sometimes known as Andrew; Anson is sometimes referred to as John or Johnnes; Rosetta is sometimes known as Roseena. In these instances I had to make a decision—usually based on the number of occurrences—to use one name over the other.

Sometimes the narrator contradicts himself in this book. At first I thought I might have to adjust the text in those instances, but ultimately I felt that Mr. Still was usually doing this on purpose, that this was another example of his brilliance at examining the strange wonder of memory. For example, early on the narrator says that he "was not shy," but later on he assures the reader that he *was* shy. Perhaps this is a commentary on memory, especially childhood memory, when we tend to let a particular thing about ourselves suit the situation. This, to me, reveals Mr. Still's deep and generous honesty about being a child, about memory, about the operations of the heart and soul. Mr. Still understood the beauty and absolute complexity of human beings.

One of the major changes I made to the book was to title it *Chinaberry*. Sometimes the pages of this manuscript were marked with "Gone to Texas" at the top of the page, but I was still not sure if this was what Mr. Still had intended for the title or not. Once I had finished editing the book, however, it was clear to me that the title needed to be *Chinaberry*, because the so-named ranch becomes a sort of magical place for the narrator, timeless and representative of much more than his time in Texas. Chinaberry is also the narrator's whole childhood, his entire life. Chinaberry is his memory and grief and joy.

We each have our own Chinaberry.

I felt the word suggested innocence, even the loss of innocence. I also loved the image of the chinaberry trees on the ranch, which Mr. Still mentions throughout. Like the narrator, the chinaberry tree is tough and resilient and a stranger in a strange land, having been brought to the United States from Asia, much like the boy is brought from Alabama to Texas.

I rewrote the entire manuscript on my own laptop to give myself a better feel for the words, for the rhythm, for the perfection of Mr. Still's language. Piecing this book together often felt like constructing a wonderful quilt that was all there, even though the pieces had been mixed together in a deep basket. The chapters, as he had written them, were not in any discernible order, but while going through his papers (which his daughter, Teresa, generously shared with me), I happened upon a hastily written outline. Mr. Still had jotted down on a legal pad the order in which he wanted this story told for the first several chapters. I have put them in the order he wished and guessed at the order for the remaining chapters, which were easier to place because of chronological hints within the text. This ordering was made much easier because of the earlier work of two friends of Mr. Still, Carol Boggess and Sam Linkous, who first reviewed the handwritten manuscript and spent many hard hours typing it simply because they loved his writing.

Among the people who knew Mr. Still, there is much debate about whether or not this book is true. He often told similar versions of the story to many of his confidants, and even to people he had recently met and had taken an immediate liking to. While I worked on this book, at least a dozen people related to me their memories of Mr. Still's sharing the story with them. Some felt it was outright fiction, and others were certain his tale was word-for-word memoir. The bottom line is that we have no way of knowing if this is memoir or fiction. I believe it is a more powerful book because of that mystery. There seems to be one thing that is incontestable: *Chinaberry* is at least rooted in some deep essential truth, which is at the heart of all the best writing. When writers give advice to "write what you know," they are not necessarily telling you to tell your life story so much as they are saying that writers ought to tell their own essential truth. Whether this book is memoir or fiction, Mr. Still's truth lives within it. The wonderful messiness of real life exists in these pages, and the characters become real people to us, whether they were or not.

There are some things within the book that are undeniably autobiographical. Woven throughout this tale of Texas is also a lovely ode to Mr. Still's birth-state of Alabama, as well as a careful tribute to his parents, whose love was large if not demonstrative, something he wrote and talked about freely. The narrator's father is a veterinarian, or "horse doctor," to use Mr. Still's description of his own father's profession. Like the narrator, Mr. Still had a short-lived stint as the first boy in the family and was doted upon by his many sisters. In his brief autobiographical writing (*Contemporary Authors Autobiography Series*, vol. 17 [Detroit: Gale Research, 1993]), Mr. Still wrote this about his childhood: "Sometimes I tell folk I was born in a cotton patch as one of my first memories is of running about with a small sack Mama had sewed up for me." He echoes these lines in chapter 1 of *Chinaberry*, when the narrator says the following: "Later in life I would joke that I was born in a cotton patch, but sometimes I felt as if I had been, for my first memories are of running along the rows of cotton, picking a boll here and there. By the time I could walk, my mother had sewn up a muslin sack for me." There was an actual, known family connection to Texas, as his parents had homesteaded there before his birth, just as the narrator's had, and the narrator's father "never got Texas out of his mind." When he was five, Mr. Still and his family moved in with his grandparents near Hootlacka Creek, which the narrator mentions as a place where he had picked flowers with his sisters. Likewise, Mr. Still wrote in his autobiography of a "black wet nurse" named Fanny, "who helped Mama care for us. She diapered us, comforted us, shielded us. We loved her with all our hearts." She shows up in *Chinaberry* as the narrator's wet nurse: "There was one, Aunt Fanny, who had helped my mother care for the ten children as they arrived. Diapering, and diaper washing, seemed to be her chief employment, along with quieting whines and rocking infants to sleep." Mr. Still says nothing in his autobiographical writing of having gone to Texas as a teenager, however. In fact, he skips over his teenage years almost completely.

All of the best writers use their own lives in some way. And Mr. Still was surely one of the best.

Chinaberry is an ode to storytelling, since we learn an equal amount about the dead and the invisible characters in this story as we do about the ones involved in the present action, and all these tales are related to us by way of stories being told around the farm, whether they be Lurie's quiet recollections as she lunches with the narrator beneath the chinaberry trees or the tales Anson delivers in his boisterous way on the swing during a hot summer night.

And *Chinaberry* is certainly complex, with some puzzlements for readers. What exactly are Anson and his wife up to, anyway? How does the narrator really feel about all of this? Each reader will read the book in a different way, of course. The most brilliant thing is that Mr. Still allows the reader that power, and he refused to let things be easily resolved. He knew that real life is complex, so writing must be as well. Mr. Still allowed his characters to speak for themselves, and for that reason I will not share any of my own judgments on what all is happening here beneath the surface, between the lines. But there is much going on in those hidden, secret places. This book proves that Mr. Still was a master of the subtle, a position that most writers can only hope to achieve. It seems to me that in this book Mr. Still has hidden as many things as he has revealed, and those secret things hunched in shadows are just as beautiful and complicated as those that he chose to illuminate.

No matter, as Mr. Still often said. The most important thing is that *Chinaberry* is a wonderful, lovely piece of art. In fact, I think it is even more wonderful because it is a great mystery. I like to think that Mr. Still would have enjoyed the fact that no one really knows whether this book is true. We do not know, but we do know that each reader is able to decide for himself or herself. This is one of the many gifts Mr. Still has given us with *Chinaberry*. As one of the earliest readers of this manuscript, as the person who had the great honor of editing the story, and as a writer who was taught by a master to discover something new every day and then to think intently about it, I know what I believe.

There are also several quotes Mr. Still wrote down within the *Chinaberry* papers that lead me to believe that he was playing with the notions of memory and memoir, of fiction and essential truth, while writing this book. Chief among them are these: "When you die others who think they know you will concoct things about you. . . . Better pick up a pen and write it yourself, for you know yourself best," by Sholom Aleichem; "Of course

one must make allowance for the tendency to heighten and co-
lour memories," by Professor Tinker in *James Boswell's London
Journal 1762-1763*; and "How does a man—be he good or bad—
big or little—. . . make his memories interesting?" by Augustine
Birrell in *Obiter Dicta*. Mr. Still jotted down many other similar quotes among his *Chinaberry* papers. There were also many
magazine articles about the way memory can play tricks on us,
about the way we sometimes transform childhood memories to
be what we want them to be.

I have chosen two quotations from among his papers to be
on the frontispiece of this book. The Lillian Hellman comment
about childhood was written on a sheet of paper surrounded by
Mr. Still's notes on Texas. His own comment about reality was
scrawled on a sheet of paper all by itself, as if he had set it apart
to open the book. Both seem appropriate for a story involving
tender childhood memories interwoven with the wisdom of an
old man. Likewise, I chose another of Mr. Still's scrawled notes
to serve as the last line for *Chinaberry*, since it seems to sum up
everything he was trying to show: "I grew up; I remembered."
Isn't this what every artist is doing, in one way or another? For
writers are nothing without the remembering.

Throughout my editing of this manuscript it seemed very
clear to me that Mr. Still wanted, more than anything, to tell the
truth in this book while also leaving some mystery behind. The
truth, of course, is nothing less than the human condition, and
conveying it is a tall order for any writer. That's exactly what the
haunting ending does. I believe the last chapter of this book is
right up there with the five or six best endings of all time, dripping with perfection.

While editing this remarkable book, I was moved and
changed. Mr. Still's writing is so beautiful and rhythmic and
precise that it made me more excited about being a writer my-

self. This book affected me to the core, for it is more than a record of three months in Texas during the narrator's childhood. It is a history of his entire life's thought process. It is a record of a place and time gone with the hot and ever-present Texas winds. It is a collection of stories about people who mattered, who are gone except in the memories of those who loved them and in these pages. Mr. Still has given them all to us in this wonderful last gift he left behind. He has given us his narrator (and, by extension, himself), along with Anson, Lurie, his parents, Ernest, the Knuckleheads—all of them—and once met, they will change and move you, too.

I am so thankful to Teresa Reynolds for trusting me to work on this project, and I deeply respect the fierce loyalty she has to Mr. Still and his legacy. I also appreciate the faith in me that Mr. Still's literary advisers, Bill Marshall, Lee Smith, and Bill Weinberg, exhibited when they asked me to edit this book. I cannot begin to thank Lee Smith, in particular, for all the ways she has helped to make me a better writer, teacher, parent, and person. This book would also not exist without the determination and intelligence of Laura Sutton, who understands what an important text this is for Appalachian literature. Everyone at the University Press of Kentucky also deserves praise for ushering this book into the world and for making sure it was presented in the most beautiful way possible. I dedicate my work on this project to Mike Mullins, the director of the Hindman Settlement School, who loved Mr. Still and who is loved by many himself.

CHAPTER one

Gone to Texas

THIS WAS A PLACE where half the world was sky, a place I had never imagined, much less expected to be. We had passed through Waco the day before, heading west, looking for work. The cotton fields we had passed thus far had only begun to whiten, and until now there had been no market for our services.

We numbered four. Our leader was Ernest, a widower in his late thirties who had been here before, under similar circumstances. There were two young men, Cadillac and Rance, both in their twenties, called "the Knuckleheads" by Ernest, and for good reason. And I was thirteen, barefoot, in simple garments: a shirt my mother had made for me and a pair of bib overalls.

We stood on a dusty corner near the courthouse in the beating sun. Several men wandered out to us, looking us over. One spat and said, "You're a week too early. My crop's not quite ready. A week from now I can use you. In fact, I'll need you." He stayed, looking at us, speculating, I suppose, that enough cotton in his field was ready for a first picking. And it could be that was why he stayed on and was joined by a couple of other men. One of them approached and stood watching us, too. He was not a farmer, as could readily be seen by his way of dressing. He was sharply dressed in cowboy boots and the kind of hat that I would later learn was generally worn by cattlemen.

I stood there in the dust with the edges of my straw hat pulled down to further shade my face. My straw had a hole in it, and I suppose a tuft of hair was sticking out. My heels were rusty, for I had gone barefoot all summer, and every summer, and I suppose my elbows were likewise. There were ten of us children at home, and though my mother took a wet rag to the ground-in dirt on my neck every day and insisted my feet be washed before bedtime, there was no such thing as whitening my sunburned feet. I glanced down, noticing that I had a toenail hanging. I had stubbed my toe a week before, and the new nail had not quite supplanted the old one.

From the moment we had arrived in the town, the name of which has escaped me forever, I was aware of the many horses. Saddle horses were hitched to a row of posts before and behind the courthouse, and there was a post or two before every store. As I have always been aware of birds, I recollect the sparrows washing themselves in the dust, pecking at the horse apples strewn along the square.

The man in the boots came closer, walked up to me, and said: "Howdy, Little Man." I glanced at him and managed to say "Hey," which was so small a sound it barely escaped my lips. As the man stared at me, I moved closer to Ernest. My father had entrusted me to Ernest, and he had kept an eye to my comfort all the way from Alabama. Keeping an eye on me consisted of seeing mainly that the mischievous Knuckleheads did not play tricks on me as they did on each other. He made sure that I had all I wanted to eat, that the trip was halted when I was thirsty. He took care that the bed of a quilt and hard pillow I had brought along was well placed in the churchyards and on the lumber piles we had slept upon on the way out. My bed was always at least within six feet of his, a bar against fear in the dark and homesickness.

I had turned thirteen in the middle of the month before. And more independent of others than a child of my age might have been expected to be. A brother had "kicked me out of the cradle" almost within the year of my own birth, and I suppose I had been denied the nurturing most Southern children received. From the moment I could walk, I was treated as an adult.

I did not lack for love, but it was undemonstrative. My mother loved me fiercely, but I remember her kissing me only once, and I recall my embarrassment. To my recollection I never sat on my father's knee. But he took me with him everywhere he went. And he listened to me. Papa was a veterinarian—or rather a "horse doctor," which is a veterinarian without formal training.

I ought to mention here my size. Although I was thirteen, I was taken for something like six. I was the only child in the first grade who had had to stand on a pencil box to reach the blackboard. The same was true of my baby brother, Alfred, yet in time we both took off physically, in our later teens.

Still, the booted man stood before us. I realized that he did not seem wilted by the heat like everyone else. He seemed as fresh as morning, neat in figure, in dress. His belt bore a buckle with a bull's head in silver. His khaki pants bore a crease. His shirt was white, in contrast to those of his fellows, and where a tie might have been he kept a handkerchief. Any practiced eye might have ascertained that here was a man who had a wife behind him who cared about his appearance, and there was a certain affluence to support it. Yet he was in working clothes. He wore two wedding bands, one gold and one platinum, on his ring finger.

What he was doing in this town on that day I do not know. As I later learned, he certainly did not need cotton pickers. His farm was in the next county, and he had Mexican families living on the place who took care of the livestock and also assisted in the house, yard, and barn.

This man stood apart. He was Anson Winters. One of the farmers asked, "Anson, what are you doing here?"

His reply bore an element of both facetiousness and directness: "The same as you. Attending to my own business."

The inquirer laughed with some amount of embarrassment. He knew this man, for he had a certain fame in the region, enjoyed a certain admiration from all who knew him. They knew his ordeal, which had not entirely passed.

Later, I asked him how he happened to be in that town on that day, a town in another county, a town where he had no business connections, and he said, "This is going to be hard to believe. But bear with me, it is a fact. I was looking for you. I was looking for a boy to fit into the place of my son. Yet it's not too strange when you know I've been looking for several years for you. I believed you were somewhere. I had to believe it to keep my head steady. I had to look. Looking made it possible to bear the ache."

His first wife had died in childbirth, in the first year of their marriage. The infant, a boy, had not been expected to live. But he did. The only explanation ever given to me, and not by the father, was that he was "afflicted." A bright, beautiful child, they said, with a "breathing problem." The child had asthma attacks that would have been fatal had not he had his father to work with his chest, breathe into his mouth, and bring life back to him. The child lived for six years and never learned to walk without support.

For six years Anson entrusted the child to no one, not even to Anson's own mother, who often pleaded with him to let her rear her grandson. Anson was in literal physical contact day and night for six years, at night with a forefinger hooked into the child's navel, the palm of his hand spread across the small chest to monitor his breathing. He carried the child with him everywhere. He was never out of hearing, or as I was told, more than three minutes away from it.

Folk remembered seeing him galloping on his bay mare, babe in arms.

And then the child died. Anson had to be restrained in bed for three days.

Of course I didn't know any of that then, standing in the sun in that courthouse square. But something about his face spoke these things to me, even if I didn't realize it at the time.

Anson's gray-blue eyes never wandered from mine as he asked Ernest what he could do for us. Yes, he said, he had cotton to be picked, and it was only beginning to open. He'd even house us and charge us with no board.

He glanced down at my feet and inquired about my sore toe.

"I stubbed it," I said. Being my father's first son, I was not shy. "It don't hurt."

At last his eyes lit on Ernest, who accepted readily. Always on the lookout for me, he said, "This boy needs a drink of water."

"Come on, I'll buy you soda waters," said Anson.

"Soda water won't do it," Ernest replied. "Just water."

The drinking water we had encountered for the last few days had been alkaline, next to undrinkable, and did little to quench thirst.

Anson led us inside the courthouse to a fountain stoked with ice, which made the water more palatable. Even had I been as tall for my age as I should have been, I couldn't have stretched up to drink. Anson lifted me, and as I put my mouth to the squirt of water, he began to tremble. He set me down quickly. "Not too much cold water at one time," he said. He lifted me again. He again trembled, but he held me until I had my fill.

"You fellows need something to eat?" Anson asked Ernest.

"We're making out," Ernest said. He was not one for charity or pity, but he did know how to do business. "What about some cotton sacks?"

"We've got all sizes at the house," Anson replied. "Except maybe for this boy."

He went into the store and bought a yard of duck fabric, and on returning he asked me if I had ever picked before.

Later in life I would joke that I was born in a cotton patch, but sometimes I felt as if I had been, for my first memories are of running along the rows of cotton, picking a boll here and there. By the time I could walk, my mother had sewn up a muslin sack for me, one that hung by a strap around my neck and reached just below the knee. My father always promised I could go to the gin with him when enough was harvested to make a bale, so I picked as fast as I could. I recollect that my sisters would never hoe or chop cotton within sight of the road. For a girl to be seen laboring in the fields was against the mores of the times. Yet they all did it, out of sight, my sisters and female cousins. Even mama, on top of her chores of cooking, laundry, scrubbing, and bed making, used to come to the fields in late afternoon and help until sunset. Mama was not afraid of acquiring a freckle on her nose or a tan on her cheeks and wore no protective clothing. My sisters worked swathed in straw hats, their arms deep in cotton stockings, collars standing on end to shield necks, their faces bathed in a screening of cow's cream.

To Anson's inquiry as to whether I had experienced picking cotton, I was too awed to make a verbal reply. I nodded yes.

And when he emerged from a store with the duck for a sack, he brought with him a cone of ice cream, which had always been a rarity in my life, chiefly for the lack of ice to freeze it. To be handed a cone on that day, with the thermometer in the upper

nineties, went far toward breaking down my natural resistance
to any overture by a stranger.

The Knuckleheads looked so hungrily at the ice cream that
Anson went back into the store and returned with three cones.
Ernest refused his, so I ended up eating two. Ernest had a certain distrust of the obviously affluent. During the whole of this
chance encounter, the Knuckleheads kept hunting the shady
spots beneath the elms. The only jobs they had ever held were
in a cotton mill at Shawmut, delivering bobbins in the spinning
room. Any strong sunlight, in either Alabama or Texas, was an
abomination to them.

"Need any branch water in your car?" Anson asked, and Ernest indicated we might need a gill. Our car's tank was directly
filled to the brim.

I had expected this cowboy to be riding a horse, but it turned
out he was driving an Overland. It was his wife's machine. I'd
never heard of a woman owning a car. The car was as spotless as
the driver. No mud on the fenders, windshields clean. This was
in marked contrast to our Model T Ford, which was crusted with
the mud of the four states we had crossed.

"The boy can ride with me," Anson suggested.

"He'll stay with us," Ernest replied, true to his mandate from
Papa to keep me under his eye.

We had hardly started off, keeping our distance from the
Overland to avoid the raised dust, when Rance leaned in close
and said, "Boy, have you got it *made*! That big shot was eating
you up with his eyes."

"You can put rocks in your cotton sack when you weigh in,
and he'll let you by with it," Cadillac added.

"We'll just work for this man," Ernest said, soberly, "and have
nothing else to do with him."

"Tell you what," Cad said, "let's pick enough white stuff to buy gas and then get the hell back to Alabama."

"What I say," agreed Rance. "I don't want to stay where the water tastes like horse piss."

Both were beginning to have the feeling of being lost, which always precedes genuine homesickness.

"You'll harden up," Ernest said. "We intend to be here awhile." Ernest had in mind trying out Texas with a view to settling down. It was already in his head, I was later to learn, to take the three of us back home should any permanent job turn up. Not cotton picking, which was seasonal. Ernest had several talents. Back home in Alabama, he had been living with a daughter and her husband, since his wife had been dead some ten years. Of his unworthy son-in-law, he had remarked to my father, "When he comes in the front door, I go out the back."

How Ernest happened to take me along was that my father had loaned him some money for expenses in exchange for my experiencing Texas. Papa had once lived in Texas, and it had never gotten out of his blood. He wanted me to know what it was like, and it wouldn't hurt that I would be making some money along the way.

Why Ernest allowed the Knuckleheads to accompany us was a mystery even to himself and often exclaimed about along the way. They too probably furnished a few dollars and offered some companionship in a strange territory. Ernest and Cadillac and Rance hadn't been anywhere much. I'd barely been out of Chambers County, Alabama. And here we were on a real adventure in this world made up of half sky.

We had long left the swamps and lush landscape of East Texas, and as we followed the Overland there was nothing the eye could hit up against. It was a land without features, flat as a pancake, cotton fields stretching to the earth's edge. Dust rose in a red cloud behind us. How far we traveled I can't say. It took fully an hour, and in those days thirty-five miles an hour was rated as a fast clip. Whereas the main road went straight as a pencil, we were soon off it and on a narrower new road that meandered from farm to farm.

We had left all signs of habitation when a low, rambling homestead appeared ahead. A lane some couple hundred yards in length began where stood a mailbox bearing the legend *A. W. Winters*. I noted the mailbox. It was to be my link to home.

Back home, in August our Alabama yard was half-filled with petunias, brown-eyed Susans, and gaillardias. I was used to a place that possessed a cape jasmine by the step, which needed only a bucket of cold water thrown on it to sweeten the air. But here there were hitching posts, horse apples scattered about, two great live oaks shading a corner of the house, and a clump of chinaberry trees—which gave the farm its name, Chinaberry—sheltering a wooden contraption of a swing, and a single pomegranate tree hanging with fruit, surrounded by a protecting fence. This was horse country. Farmers owning vehicles other than wagons were few. But there were two trucks parked in a side yard, one a cattle truck with high siding bespeaking the prosperity of the farm. The Winters cotton farm was the size of any three properties thereabouts.

Anson drew up at the front steps, and Ernest pulled alongside. There on the porch stood Lucretia Winters, known as Lurie. She was somewhat surprised by her husband's return at midday, by now this being about one o'clock in the afternoon. As you could hear a car coming a mile away, she had been warned and had put on a fresh gingham dress and white shoes, and her corn-silk hair was loose about her shoulders. If flowers were missing in the yard, there was a human blossom on the porch.

Lurie: she was as beautiful as my mother.

Ernest gasped, the Knuckleheads stared, and from that moment, all of Ernest's defenses were down. He made no objection when Anson reached into the car beside him, lifted me out, and carried me to the porch.

"Sandspurs are rough on the feet," he explained. I was suddenly aware of my rusty ankles and elbows, my smudged face, which hadn't been properly washed in a week, and my dirty ears, within which my mother would have said birds had been roosting.

Anson smelled of Lucky Tiger, the lotion barbershops used to dispense. I was embarrassed by being carried at my age, so I wriggled, thinking he might put me down. Cadillac and Rance would have a good laugh over this. But he didn't.

"Heavy," I said.

"As a chicken feather," Anson replied, and he gave his wife a peck on the cheek.

Later, Ernest remarked that had this been his woman he'd have shown more ardor.

Anson and Lurie

LURIE HAD FIRST laid eyes on Johnnes Anson Winters when she was twelve, and she had resolved to marry him or not marry at all. So she decided to wait for him. There was not a woman in the counties thereabouts, it was commented, who wouldn't abandon spouse and offspring should the opportunity have blossomed to be his second wife after the death of his first one. He was known, after all, as that cowboy who had carried his afflicted son in his arms from birth until his death at the age of six. The memory of Anson on horseback with a thumb in the baby's mouth for a pacifier stirred hearts.

Anson was the second son of Big Jack Winters, owner of the Bent Y Ranch in one county and half a section of cotton land in another adjoining. The cotton farm was tended by Mexican sharecroppers, with Anson as their casual overseer. Anson insisted on living on the old home place where his father had taken up land in the last years of the past century. This despite the distance he had to drive to the Towerhouse, the name he used to refer to the main house of the ranch and its operations. None of the three brothers were any longer cowboys, and they engaged in various activities along with the affairs of the Bent Y.

Anson's two brothers, Jack and Bronson, operated a farm each, with hired help, on land in the vicinity of the ranch. They raised hay and millet and corn; they reared horses for the re-muda; and they sold the surplus of forage and grain and saddle stock. The Bent Y was a family cooperative, shared by its members. No authority was wrested from Big Jack, only supplemented. Now in his eighties, a bit uncertain on his feet, his word was law, and nobody wished otherwise.

In earlier days, before he had left West Tennessee, where he had migrated from North Carolina, Big Jack Winters had married a widow some years his elder, who had not only a half-grown son, Bronson, but also a sizable acreage of rich land bordering on the Mississippi River. In those pioneer days, women wore out like a cake of soap, and the widow was said to have died within a few months. At her passing, Big Jack sold the land for a sizable amount and headed west, Bronson in tow. He took up land in Texas under the Homestead Act and grew cotton until the windfall of the Towers Ranch came his way. He had the gold certificates in hand to make the deal when the odd chance presented itself. Anson told me his father had said those were the wild years, with claims and counterclaims, and a man's life was in constant danger. Every man carried a gun as commonly as he packed a pocketknife.

In due course, Big Jack married the woman I was to be coached to call grandma, a woman near half his age. Bronson's age. It was not easy to say "Grandma." I had to squeeze it out at first. I already had one live grandma back home in Alabama, and the other one had passed on.

Because of the striking resemblance of Anson and Jack to their foster brother, Bronson, I long mistook him for their father. Neither had inherited the physical characteristics nor the brittle personality of Big Jack. Lest I mislead, I'll allow the readers to study on this at their leisure. The Winters family was the soul of honor, their morals Victorian.

"Anson's heart is pure," Lurie told me frequently. I believe that she meant he was vulnerable. She could never forget that she had been his third choice. There had been his first wife, of course. And there was the possibility of a liaison after the death of the first wife, which haunted her.

Anson had married a childhood sweetheart after two years of college in Austin indulging in agricultural training. There had been some delay in his betrothal because he had loved two sisters and had trouble choosing between them. He was twenty-four years old.

The sisters were not twins although they appeared to be, beauties the both, dressing in identical gowns and flowered hats with veils when they appeared in public, and the pride of their father. Since they were raised in town, one would suspect they knew little firsthand of the vicissitudes faced by women living on the ranches and farms around them. The sisters were from a prosperous family who dealt in hardware. Their father had migrated from Mississippi, as their soft voices and dropped r's attested. Surnamed O'Kelly, the family had retained the O commonly dropped by most of Irish descent.

Anson's dilemma was resolved somewhat when the younger sister, Irena, began to date a clerk in her father's store. It was assumed that she had bowed in favor of her older sister, not willingly but at her father's request. Yet she did not marry the clerk or any other of the young men who paid her court for several years. And as much as Anson cherished his marriage to Melba, he did not forget Irena.

The marriage was short-lived. Melba died of childbed fever almost to the day of their first wedding anniversary. The child's breathing problems, during which he sometimes stopped breathing altogether, could only be overcome by the manual pumping of his lungs and mouth-to-mouth resuscitation, which

Anson would trust to no one else. The child, called Johnnes for his father's seldom-used first name, survived just beyond his sixth birthday.

From the day of Little Johnnes's birth, Anson no longer rode the range with his brothers. A hand was hired in his stead, and from then on Big Jack's ranch was no longer wholly a family affair. The three sons, along with their father, had developed a cattle spread from an acreage the four of them could handle in its every aspect until the acquisition of more pasture, which spread until it bordered on free range. This became too much. The operation was so large that it required employing a crew of cowboys, who spelled each other on a regular basis. Bronson and Jack soon gave up their chaps and spurs and began to develop the farms that were to consume most of their attention. The brothers met at the Towerhouse most days, heard Big Jack out, had his pronouncements translated into more practical terms by their mother, and saw to the numerous chores. To Jack fell the job of looking after the family's other business interests, including an ice-making plant in one of the towns, a feed-and-grain store, and a partnership or a large share of stocks in a bank. They also had a seasonal fertilizer operation devoted to the grinding, sacking, and distributing of phosphate, which arrived unprocessed in open railroad cars. All else was given up during cattle-shipping season.

All three brothers lived near the Towerhouse until Melba's death, upon which Anson returned to the farmstead of his birth, Chinaberry, and was undoubtedly assisted in caring for Little Johnnes by the Mexican families operating the cotton farm. Anson drove to the ranch weekdays with the baby propped on the seat beside him, and later, as he moved about mounted, the baby sat in his arms. During the first years his saddlebags were stuffed with diapers.

The countryside saw much of him, at a distance, during the six years of Little Johnnes's life, and hardly saw him at all in the years following the child's death. It was said he was even taking a hand in the cultivation of the cotton, which went against the local wisdom: "Once a cowboy, never a plowboy." But hard work is helpful in overcoming sorrow.

Although the rural telephone system was subject to frequent breakdowns, country wives kept fairly good tabs over a large area of acquaintance. But in Anson's case, little was known or could be known. His brother Jack took over the chores that involved visits to towns or any public appearances and did not relinquish them until Anson married again. On the subject of Anson, the family was mute, and they probably assumed he had had a nervous breakdown.

Lurie told me later what had happened, so far as she could find out, because she wanted me to understand Anson and not to fear him. However, we can never get plumb to the bottom of anybody, not all the way down to what is dark and hidden and cannot bear the light of recognition.

I did not understand, being only thirteen and of little experience. But I was never afraid of him. Only overawed.

And I was awed by Lurie. Beautiful Lurie. Lucretia Jeffreys, she had been. From childhood her schoolmates and townspeople called her Lurie, but she was never addressed as such by her parents or brother or sister. In Henderson, Kentucky, where both her parents were born and married, the Jeffreys were said to have some social pretensions. Bluewater, Texas, where they moved after the birth of their son, was not the place to practice them. A frontier town not too long freed from the scourge of Indian raids, Bluewater was a place where the bones of buffaloes lay whitening in the sun, where everybody came from somewhere else. The land offices were matched in number only by the saloons. Land titles were in disarray, and the disputes were sometimes settled with a gun.

Hampton Jeffreys, Lurie's father, arrived in Bluewater with a deed to a section of land that his father had bought on speculation long before. He fell into the business of real estate, which made him a rich man when the Katy Railroad came through and the land grew valuable. By the time Lurie was grown, her family did not want for anything, so her father sold off all his holdings except several dwellings and a half block of businesses and moved next door to Lurie's brother, who was some twenty years her elder and a cotton broker in Amarillo. Rent accruing from the Bluewater properties was divided between Lurie and her sister.

Her mother was forty-four when Lurie was born, and the surprise pregnancy had been an embarrassment. Her brother, who was then in college, switching between law and medicine and business administration, claimed to be ashamed. Lurie's sister, Velvet, now married to Sam Somerwell, twelve years Lurie's senior, became her de facto mother. Lurie stayed at the Somerwells as much as at home, and when her parents went to live in Amarillo, she did not follow at once. She was not to switch her interest as did her brother. She had spotted Anson when she was twelve, and the die had been cast.

The fact that Anson was five years older than her cast no weight. The clear knowledge that he was often in the company of Melba and Irena and would surely marry one of them eventually was no deterrent to her either. Velvet would point out to Lurie that Jack Winters, the brother of Anson, was nearer her own age and apparently fancy-free, and why did she not make some accommodation with him? Lurie could not say what it was about Anson that separated him from all other men, even from the brother who appeared to be cast in the same mold. Both were handsome in the rugged way a frontier town and the sun and Texas winds write on a face. She had no words to describe it until after their marriage when Anson's mother, clearly asking some indulgence for the trials her son had endured, told Lurie, "He has a pure heart." Thus Lurie's declaration of this same thing to me. It was in his eyes as in no other man's she had ever known, she said. The fact that he could not easily shake off the human contracts he had made was an earnest of it. And his mother had said, "He still has a little way to go."

The truth is, she loved him, and she finally got him, just as she had planned.

Anybody who saw Lurie at Chinaberry would have asked themselves what a woman of such carriage and personality and beauty was doing on a Texas cotton farm miles from anywhere. But she was there, and always looking fresh as rain.

Lurie had had no expectations of remaining out of touch with civilization for long. There was already a spot chosen for a house near the ranch. Anson's mother was her chief accomplice in encouraging him to leave Chinaberry to the full management of the Indian foreman, Blunt, and his extended Mexican family. Anson's mother wanted all her own family around her, and certainly none missing at the Sunday dinner table.

When Anson was absent, I was much company to Lurie, and besides welcoming me she took on the duty of explaining Anson to me as far as she could. Most of all there was the prodding to not fear him, which I never did, except once. "He suffered a traumatic loss in the death of the baby," she'd say. "He went through a terrible brain fever."

She reported that by day Anson's outward ruggedness belied the trials he had suffered. He laughed, made jokes, and trusted everybody except cottonseed buyers at the gin.

By night it was another matter. He often turned and tossed, sometimes arose and slipped into moccasins so he could walk about, to the barn or to the mailbox. Lurie would stand in the door and watch him unseen until he returned. She decided there had been some amelioration of the past except the loss of Little Johnnes. In his sleep he would mutter "My baby, my baby" or "Hold on, hold on."

She may have told me more than intended, having no one else to talk to. In her own fashion she divulged that we were both substitutes.

"You know, I heard Anson whistling yesterday for the first time," she told me, a week after my arrival. "The first time ever."

CHAPTER *Three*

Cotton Fields

WE HAD ARRIVED at siesta, that period between high noon and two when the Texas sun is at its most torrid and brightest, and the leaves of the trees hang limp and blades of the corn curl. "Nappy time," Anson dubbed it. All labor ceased. Following dinner, everybody slept or found a cool spot to await a lessening of the heat.

The sounds of our approach aroused Blunt and set him to gathering horse apples. Blunt was a full-blooded Comanche Indian. He was father and grandfather to the workers in the field and the house, having married a Mexican woman in years past, and he was a longtime guardian of Chinaberry. How close a watchdog I was to learn. I had noticed that no dog had run out to greet his master when we had first arrived at the house. In Alabama every house has a dog to bark warning at the strangers. Blunt served this purpose at Chinaberry.

While he scooped the apples into a coal scuttle with a stone shovel, he aroused two women from a hammock strung from live oaks behind the house. They were Angelica and Rosetta, who aided in the housekeeping and cooking. At Chinaberry the siesta was elongated, from eleven until four. Cotton gathering began at four in the morning and continued until dark. You can see cotton before you can see anything else, and later.

Anson had said, "We've got some hungry workers here," and that was all that was needed to set Angelica and Rosetta to cooking and Blunt to lighting a charcoal brazier. We were shown to our quarters, down a hall on the right side of the house, two doors below the parlor, which Lurie, for reasons of her own, had never entered and never would. Later I would learn that this was not from distaste, but because the parlor was sacred to her husband.

In our room there were two beds. Cadillac and Rance would occupy one, Ernest the other. A trundle bed was rolled in for me. The size of the building indicated it had once housed a family greater in size than occupied it now. Anson and Lurie rarely crossed the hall to this side of the dwelling. The house had recently been wired for lights, but the sockets were empty, awaiting a gasoline generator.

Things began to happen. The aroma of grilling steaks drifted from the yard. We were invited to clean up before the meal, to use the shower in an outbuilding directly in front of a tank fed by a windmill. The water was more than tepid. Our clothes, thrown out the door for Angelica to pick up and thrust into a gasoline-driven washing machine, were soon on the line, drying. Ernest alone had a fresh change available; the rest of us had soiled the extra pairs of bib overalls we possessed by the time we had reached the Louisiana line. These too were washed in due course.

At least our faces and hands were clean when we sat down to a table covered with a variety of foods. Even sweet potato pie, my favorite. Lurie stood by until we had our first serving, then left the room, Ernest's eyes following her as she passed the dishes and until she left us. There can be so much food that some hunger is assuaged by merely looking at it. Ernest was to remark later, "You'd of thought they knew we were coming," and

Cadillac, reading Ernest's thoughts, said, "That's some woman he's got. Who'd of figured on finding such a looker out here in the middle of nowhere?" Ernest had only grunted.

At the table Anson stood beside me, and when he saw I tasted the glass of water and rejected it, even with lumps of ice, he poured a tumbler of buttermilk for me, the summertime drink of choice in Alabama. And noting my difficulty cutting a piece from the steak, he divided it into bite-sized pieces. He even took up a fork and poked a morsel into my mouth, with Cadillac and Rance taking note the whole while. I shunned the beans and potatoes, the beets and mustard greens. As nobody counseled me to make a better choice of foods, as they would have at home, I dined mostly on pie and pound cake and pear preserves. And drank buttermilk. My thirst seemed endless.

It was no wonder that we were ready for a nap on the cool grass under the chinaberries after such a gorging. But not before the Knuckleheads got in their licks.

"Boy, have you got it made," said one.

"Got him eating out of your hand," said the other.

"If I was in your place I'd make it pay off."

Ernest added a halfhearted piece of advice. "Just watch yourself." He saw that he was losing authority.

Surfeited with food and drink as we were, we slept longer than intended. About four o'clock, Ernest waked us and said, "Let's get cracking. We're making no dough laying here." Blunt brought cotton sacks for the three of them, and Anson led me into the house for a fitting of my own sack. It was already sewed, lacking only the strap, which needed merely stitching on. Though something of a toy sack, it would drag along the ground a full yard and a half behind me, as did sacks in Texas, where rows seemed endless. A body picked until the bag was half-full, then cut off a row and picked back toward the beginning. A wagon would be there with steelyard scales to weigh the harvest.

Lurie sewed on the loop and hung it across my shoulder for measurement. Then she suddenly pressed my head against her bosom. My face tore up. I cried soundlessly, tears smearing my cheeks. I hardly knew why I cried. Because I was so far from home—from Alabama?

"My baby," Lurie breathed.

Through my tears I saw Anson's discomfort, a sudden jerking of his head so his own tears might not be seen and his leaving the room for a moment. A wound had been opened, as I was to learn. Anson and Lurie had been together three years and were childless, for whatever reason. Lurie was in her late twenties, Anson in his mid-thirties.

Blunt was waiting at the door to lead me to the fields, along with Ernest and the Knuckleheads. When Anson brought me out he hesitated. "Maybe the boy ought to stay at the house. He's already had a long day," he said.

"No longer than the rest of us," Ernest said. He was not relinquishing his mandate readily. "Young fellows can take it better than us older ones. They bounce back quicker."

The walk sliced through the fields of barely opened cotton to a farther field a half mile distant where the plants had a week's advance growth. Ahead we saw the pickers, some dozen of them, snatching at the bolls. Most of them were part of Blunt's Indian-Mexican family, the rest, other hired hands. Their arms worked like pistons. The most adept could pick up to four hundred pounds a day.

We were to work apart from this crowd, who busied the rows like a swarm of bees feeding on clover. We chose a set of rows and began. For me, it was as if I'd never left the business; with the others it was an awkwardness gradually overcome. To pick a boll of cotton would seem not to be difficult, as it is not. The point is cotton weighs like air, next to nothing, and pays a cent a pound, so elbows must fly. And there is an art to snatching the locks without puncturing the cuticles of your fingers on the dry sharp point of the boll. I had acquired this art. Cadillac and Rance and Ernest had bleeding fingers within a half hour. And there was the sun beating down even at five in the evening, apparently refusing to set, and there was the headache breeze fanning across the land. That half hour convinced the three of them that our stay at Chinaberry had to be short, that we should move on as soon as we could raise a stake of money enough for grub and gasoline. And to replace all four tires, which were slick as a pool ball. The transmission had also been acting up.

The pickers strode back and forth to the wagon, where the waiting baskets were filled with cotton, then weighed and dumped. The three of us together—the Knuckleheads and I— had not yet filled a single basket. I was performing with the best of them, if not better, but still we hadn't gathered much.

We saw Anson approaching at a distance on his saddle horse, Blue. Blue was a roan, her name at odds with her coat. The identifying number at the auction where she was purchased had been stamped in azure paint on her rump.

On a Texas afternoon with the air like glass, you can see farther than any place earthly, and the man and his horse appeared long before they drew up at the wagon.

Anson set a glass jug—full of lemonade and wrapped in burlap—on the wagon and hitched Blue to the wagon wheel. He strode out to us, walking beside me and dropping cotton into my sack.

The three of us had not a dry thread on us and the water was dripping from our noses. Anson's face was dry as a hat. Not a bead of sweat dampened his brow.

Anson sauntered away down the row, an imposing silhouette against the white sky.

"Don't that man ever sweat?" Rance whispered.

In the field, a jackrabbit sprang up and hopped away, in not too much of a hurry.

"Gosh dog!" the Knuckleheads said as one.

Being only familiar with the cottontails back home in Alabama, we were astounded. It was as if a mouse had become as large as a cat.

"Them ears!" said one.

"Big as a calf!" said the other.

Ernest was less impressed. The sun beating down and the prospect of the endless rows of cotton before us would have dampened any elation. Lifting his hat, he rubbed a hand across his head back to front where the hair was thinning, and the gathered sweat came off in a shower.

"If you Knuckleheads don't get to work, you'll be *eating* jackrabbits," Ernest said. We were so stuffed with food from Anson's table that it made the work all the more laborious. To the right of us, the pickers were cleaning up the cotton, working like machines, elbows flying, hands snatching.

I got drowsy and yearned to take a nap. The heat was like a curtain we moved through, our motions dulled and heavy.

My drowsiness grew.

"You're getting too hot," Anson said, appearing beside me as if out of the blue. "Let's go to the wagon, get you a drink of lemonade, rest awhile."

I followed. He poured me the cold lemonade. The alkaline taste of the water surmounted even the lemon juice and the sweetening. It tasted like medicine. But it was cold.

I sat in the shade of the wagon, and I could not keep my eyes open. Anson had not spoken. Now he said, "Sleepy sleep. Sleepy sleep." Those were the two words I was to hear nightly in the future, when I started sleeping in his room.

I slept, and when I wakened, the sun had lowered a bit. Cicadas cried out. I was bathed in perspiration, and Anson was fanning me with his hat. My cotton sack had little more than a wad of cotton inside, but he had shoved it under my head. There was not a dry thread on me, despite Anson's fanning.

When I opened my eyes, Anson peered down at me. "Little Man, let's go to the house," he said. Then he called to Ernest, "I'm taking this boy to the house. The heat is getting to him."

Ernest, with a sweep of his hand, indicated go ahead.

The Knuckleheads had stopped picking and were watching us. I saw their mouths working and knew what one of them was saying: "This makes my tail cut cordwood."

But before Anson lifted me into the saddle, he picked me up and hung me by the galluses of my overalls on the steelyards, weighing me as he might a sack of cotton. He trembled, and he trembled again swinging me up onto the horse's back.

"Sixty-nine pounds and thirteen years old," he remarked. "We need to put some pounds on you." And then, "Are you right sure you're thirteen?"

I said I was right sure.

"Let's say you're six," he said. "To me, you're six."

I didn't respond. I didn't know then that he had had a child who had died at that age. Little Johnnes.

Now at last he asked my name. I told him. He studied me a moment.

He was never to address me by it.

CHAPTER four

Discovering Chinaberry

WE WERE TO only have that one day in the cotton fields. Anson hadn't needed us in the first place.

On our second day at Chinaberry, he had other jobs for us. Having already apprized Ernest's experience in the livery trade, he proposed that Ernest work with the horses at the ranch, in part to spell himself. That way, at least until fall roundup, he'd have more time at home. Cadillac and Rance were hired to deliver ice in drays to houses in a town some dozen miles away, starting from an ice plant the Winters family owned. All leapt at the chance of doing otherwise than they were now doing. Particularly Ernest, who saw a chance for higher-class employment.

"Now you Knuckleheads won't have to pop another sweat," Ernest said to Cadillac and Rance. "And you can eat all the ice you want."

In hindsight, I believe that when he first laid eyes on the four of us, the wheels were already turning in Anson's head. In things that mattered to him, he was fast on the draw. The second morning of our stay, I woke up and found that Ernest was already off to the ranch and the Knuckleheads were gone to the ice plant. Anson had preceded Ernest in a truck, Ernest following. Blunt had taken the boys in the pickup truck. Ernest had apparently abandoned his mandate, aware that I was in more caring hands than his own. And he had been told about Blunt and his long-time career as guardian of Anson and Jack in childhood, so he figured Blunt would become my shadow as well.

I waked in that far room at Chinaberry, alone. The house had blinds rather than shades, and they were half-open, the sun already high outside. I heard doves calling. And I had hardly cracked my eyes before Lurie was standing in the door with a pan of water, a washrag floating in it, and in her other hand a goblet of water with a floating lump of ice. Even with my taste buds dulled by the ice, the water was just barely drinkable.

Lurie set the pan down on a bureau, looked into the chamber pot by the bed, and finding it empty, pointed to it and withdrew. I jumped out of bed, used the pot, and pushing it under the boards, climbed back in. I was sleeping in the single nightshirt I had with me. Lurie returned, pulled back the sheet, and set about washing my face and neck, not neglecting my ears. She examined my feet ruefully. I had washed the surface dirt from them the night before, and Ernest had torn a strip from a clean handkerchief and anchored the unshed toenail anew. My rusty heels and ankles shamed me.

"We'll do something about that toe tonight," she said, more to herself than to me, and finishing the task, she pressed my head against her breast and sighed. "Put your clothes on and come to breakfast."

She sashayed out of the room, leaving her scent behind her. She smelled of violets. How often had I gone with my sisters to pick violets in our pasture along Hootlacka Creek. The source of this fragrance, which pervaded her presence, was a bottle of perfume, Violet Spring, on her dressing table. And the smell that clung to Anson was from a beaker of Lilac Vegetal after-shave lotion on the shelf where his shaving mug and long razor were kept.

Then I saw on a chair at the foot of the bed my bib overalls and shirt, freshly laundered and ironed. I wore no underclothes, a lack soon remedied. And there was a pair of moccasins for me, a perfect fit, made overnight by Blunt from a single piece of leather, not single-tack-driven but bound together by thongs.

At the table I discovered cornflakes. A bowl of them sat on my plate, floating in milk and sweetened. My first taste. I added three more spoons of sugar. I ate a second bowl of cereal when it was offered and would have downed a third had I not been ashamed. The scrambled eggs and bacon I hardly nibbled. I did eat a biscuit in sampling the three varieties of jam—fig, blackberry, and pear. This kind of diet would have been commented on by Anson, yet Lurie said not a word.

In the kitchen behind us, Angelica and Rosetta were laughing. Anson often said they were probably born laughing. Their voices were a mixture of Spanish and English, although both could speak English almost without accent. Their families were the only Mexicans I was to see, and I was never to see a black person there. There was a black cowpuncher on Big Jack's ranch, but I never saw him. In Alabama, the black folk were everywhere, and there was one, Aunt Fanny, who had helped my mother care for the ten children as they arrived. Diapering, and diaper washing, seemed to be her chief employment, along with quieting whines and rocking infants to sleep. When my mother, with her many housekeeping chores, had no time to cure a hurt or answer a question, Aunt Fanny did.

As for Rosetta's and Angelica's amusement, Anson was to say, "Don't ask what's so funny. They don't know themselves." Once these young women had cleaned up the kitchen, Rosetta was off to change the sheets and pillowcases on the beds, which was done every day, sweep the floors, and dust; and Angelica had the gasoline-powered washing machine going to launder everything. From day to day, I never wore a garment twice if it was unwashed. After these chores, Angelica and Rosetta were off to do their own tasks at their homes, and they were back again at four to cook supper. The kitchen stove was not fired again until supper, to spare the house the heat. At noon Lurie and I snacked, the two of us, on pimento sandwiches, cold chicken or ham, and I drank buttermilk while she drank iced tea.

That second day seemed short, as I had some exploring to do. I looked into all of the nine rooms except the one that was kept locked. The bathroom was two rooms down from Lurie and Anson's bedroom. The tub was huge and rested on four claw-like legs. Until adjustments were employed, I couldn't reach the chain that released the water into the commode or sit on the commode without my feet dangling, and sitting presented some danger of falling in. This was to be remedied soon. I used the shower in the washhouse, an act required of me morning and mid-afternoon in hot weather.

That first free day at Chinaberry, I saw most of what there was to see. Anson's saddle horse, Blue, had a companion, Red, the horse Lurie rode. Red was red, a matching roan. I climbed up the ladder in the barn and looked; I peered into the cotton house, where a mountain of it was stored, awaiting the gin. There was the garden where grew the vegetables now beginning to wither in the heat. I discovered the flowers that Lurie could not grow in the yard or on the porch. They were in the garden. When she tried to have them on the porch or yard, they were only destroyed. Once, a pony had climbed the steps and eaten those in pots.

All during my exploration, Blunt followed me.

I tried out the hammock under the cool shade of the china-berries and then sat in the two-seated wooden swing. It required someone sitting opposite to balance the weight. Blunt came and sat down across from me, and we rocked back and forth awhile. I didn't know what to say, and he said nothing. Lastly, I revisited the cotton fields, near enough to the pickers to hear the drone of their voices.

When Anson returned from his work that afternoon and asked for a report on my day, I couldn't get my mouth open. He was as yet too much a stranger to speak with freely. That too was soon to be remedied.

Lurie had something to report. She had been sewing up two summer shirts with sleeves ending above the elbow, and no tails. There were buttons, yet to fasten only one or none at all was accounted sufficient in hot weather. A shirt without sleeves or tails! And a pair of short underpants. They had me go into another room and put them on. Anson took one look and told Lurie, "They're too tight. They're pinching his little fixing." They were let out by sewing in a blue strip on either side. As I seemed to approve the adornment, subsequent pairs of my underpants had either blue or green piping, and Anson's as well thereafter. What he wore, I wore in a smaller version.

"We ought to do something about the boy's toe," Anson said that evening as we sat on the porch with Ernest and Lurie.

The three of them seated me in a chair. The big toe on my right foot was doused in camphor. Lurie, exercising her skill as a nurse apprentice, cut loose the hanging nail with a pair of embroidery scissors. Underneath the nail, tender to the touch, a new one was beginning to form.

I had scrubbed my feet as clean as could be, yet the heels and ankles still looked dirty. Anson said these were grass and mineral stains that would wear off. Did I know the earth we walked on was chock-full of minerals? I told him I did.

I didn't know much, except what I had overheard and what I had read in the four books that lived in my home back in Alabama. I was mostly a student of *The Cyclopedia of Universal Knowledge*. The other three books were the Holy Bible, *The Anatomy of the Horse*, and a book bought from a colporteur, *The Palaces of Sin, or The Devil in Society*.

The Bible was held in such reverence that nobody ever opened it.

The Anatomy served my father in his horse doctoring and was way too technical for me.

I had learned all I needed to know about evil from *The Palaces of Sin*. Was there not a drawing in there of a dinner party at which Jenny Manly of Alabama was standing and berating her fellow diners for drinking wine at the table? Also mentioned in this book was the drinking of gin. And the gambling with cards. And more sins.

So, *The Cyclopedia of Universal Knowledge* was my chief instrument. What did a child know of the world in those days? Only what he could hear, or observe in the fields and at the barn, and the meager knowledge gained from schoolbooks. What I knew of the world came from *The Cyclopedia*. When I had first smelled Lurie's perfume, I had known what violets signified, as well as Anson's aftershave lotion, fragrant of lilacs. "The Language of Flowers" was a chapter in my family's beloved book.

That evening I was ashamed of my dirty-looking feet. But Anson and Lurie would cure this. They had remedies for stained heels and ankles, mainly cloverine salve. Daily administrations would be applied, with my knees and elbows added to the undertaking. It worked. Gradually, with the salve at night and the wearing of moccasins by day, my feet whitened to the point that Anson picked up my foot one morning and nibbled on my toes to wake me.

That night my trundle bed was placed in the room adjoining Anson and Lurie's. Anson came in to tuck me in, and before taking the light away, he raised me for a moment to learn, he said, if I'd gained any weight since yesterday. Lurie floated in behind him, and standing with me in his arms, he drew her to us, giving me a light kiss on the chin and Lurie a fuller one on the cheek. He lowered me onto the trundle bed and said what I was to hear night after night: "Sleep good so you'll be happy in the morning. Sleepy sleep."

It seems that I cried out in the night, which I might well have done, or made disturbing sounds, for he had come with the lamp to assure me with his presence.

A routine evolved. Lurie and I were both as fresh as soap and water and clean garments could make us as we awaited Anson's return. During August, he came before sunset. As the shipping season arrived, he came later, and by October, he didn't get home until after dark.

Instead of driving to the common parking ground, he would stop in the yard, leave the motor running, jump out, and rush up the steps and embrace Lurie. Next, he would pick me up, give me a smack on the chin, then close us both in his arms, and make a groan of relief. Unused to being picked up, I felt both awkward and embarrassed, even though no fellow Alabamians were there to watch. Every time I said "I'm heavy," he would reply, "As chicken feathers." Still carrying me, he took me back to the car, and once having parked, he asked, "How was the day?" Whatever the hour, we did not have supper until he was with us.

That same second night at Chinaberry, the tick hunt was initiated, an event that would happen every night after that. In Alabama it was the red bug that was likely to burrow into the skin and fester, particularly in spots unreachable to scratch. Turpentine and kerosene and vinegar were the recommended remedies to unseat the almost-invisible insect. Usually, you scratched it free. But in Texas the tick was the problem. If allowed to hang on long enough, the tick would bloat itself with your blood and likely infect you with Rocky Mountain fever. Looking for ticks was a job for more eyes than your own. You had to be scanned top to bottom, front and back. Every day.

Here was a problem. By age twelve, boys have been imbued with the inviolability of their bodies and will not undress before anyone except their peers. Anson and Lurie worked together on this daily search, usually before bedtime. With all my clothes removed save my shorts, Lurie turned me about, looking me over carefully. She left the room, and Anson would pull my shorts down for a moment, look front and back, and jerk them up again. He'd call to Lurie, "The road's clear."

His son, having lived to only be six, did not have to pass through the insecurities of adolescence.

No matter my embarrassments, I knew that I had been taken in. Chinaberry was to be my home.

A morning came when Anson stood by my chair at the table as I devoured cornflakes and remarked, "I had a little boy once, and he used to give me a big smack every time I was going to leave him, even for a minute."

He meant a kiss. I had never kissed anybody in my life, at least not that I could remember. I looked at Lurie and her eyes said "Do it."

Anson bent down, and my mouth pressed high on his jaw. No "smack" to it.

"Huh," Anson said. "Pretty dry." Then, "Have you got a smack for Lurie?"

I did, and willingly. Hard, on the cheek.

"Good boy," said Anson.

It was a revelation.

ON THE THIRD NIGHT at Chinaberry, my bed was rolled into their bedroom, directly across from their brass bed, which in lamplight shone like gold.

Anson did not report to the ranch for the next two days. The telephone rang, some explanation was given, and on the third day, his brother Bronson arrived in a cattle truck, bringing Ernest with him, to check on us. Bronson and Anson looked so much alike that I fancied them father and son. The same sandy hair, eyes as much the true color of the sky as blue, which in different lights changed hues. Not particularly tall, but not short. The same action of knee and swing of foot. Identical clean khaki shirts, and khaki breeches tucked into polished boots. "Dirt won't stick to a Winters," I was to hear, and it seemed true enough.

Bronson shook my hand and looked me over. He plucked my chin. He knew his brother like a book, and he understood. "Come to the ranch day after tomorrow for sure," he told Anson. There was something that required his attention. Bronson let his eyes fall on me. "If they don't treat you right, come stay at my house. My children are gone, and I've a lot of empty rooms." Thus he made me welcome.

Ernest pulled me aside. "I wouldn't leave you here except you couldn't be better looked after. Too good, my opinion. Your daddy let you come along for the experience, and you're getting it. We'll stay awhile, and then I'll take you home." To that he added: "If you get too dissatisfied, you can come stay with me in the bunkhouse at the Bent Y. There's an old cowboy there will keep an eye on you. He's got more tales in him than a cat has fleas." His report on the Knuckleheads included their being reprimanded by one of the Bluewater policemen for racing their delivery wagon down the main street, resulting in breaking the axles.

Anson returned to the ranch on my fourth day at Chinaberry. That morning Lurie again appeared at my bedside with a wash pan and a washcloth. She washed the sleep from my eyes, face, and hands, and Anson brought a goblet of water with a lump of ice in it. I frowned as I swallowed the alkaline taste, and Anson said, "We'll have to do something about the water."

When he left, the house seemed very quiet. Lurie busied herself at the sewing machine making clothes for me: shirts and undershorts and wash pants. She was involved in her work, and I was alone. I had nothing but my homesickness, which burgeoned inside me.

CHAPTER five

Little Johnnes

AFTER THE PASSING of the first wife, Melba, Anson had remained at the small lying-in hospital in the county seat for two weeks helping attend to Little Johnnes, who was fighting for his life and was hardly expected to survive. Anson did not attend Melba's funeral, so precarious was the situation of their child, much to his mother-in-law's dismay.

To his father-in-law's disapproval, Irena—Melba's sister and the onetime object of Anson's affection—insisted on spending the daylight hours assisting Anson. However, the father-in-law did not forbid it, given the circumstance that the vigil was around the clock. There was no oxygen equipment, and the child could not be moved. Other physicians were brought in, one even from Austin, but after a cursory examination, they only shook their heads.

The child, given to frequent smothering spells, had to be manipulated ever so gently to start him breathing again, and on many occasions Anson snatched him from death by forcing his own breath into the boy's lungs. His mother was to say that Anson believed that by sharing his own good health with his ailing child he could save him. And he did, but for six years only.

For those first two weeks, Anson sat beside the baby by day, tiny hand in his own, his eyes hardly straying from the child's face. Little Johnnes lay half-somnolent, his flesh a cast of blue from lack of oxygen. By night, Anson lay right beside the baby. Irena brought food and drink from home, food she herself had prepared and which, it was said, she actually had to spoon into his mouth, so great was his reluctance to eat. Though there were a cook and a washerwoman who served her parents' household, Irena also saw that Anson had fresh clothes, washed and ironed by her own hand. Such was the news that leaked to the wide country-side, which thrived on such personal tidbits. The wisdom by tele-phone was that, despite religious injunctions against a brother-in-law marrying a sister-in-law and the expected objections of Irena's parents, these two would turn up on a Saturday after-noon in a clerk's office in some courthouse and be married. And it would be as if nothing had happened, except in the case that the child did survive, Irena would be there to share in his care.

This was assumed despite the known fact that Irena was now engaged to a lawyer in the town, a lawyer of good family and rising promise. She even wore a diamond engagement ring. To confuse the issue, the young lawyer himself often stopped by the hospital, stood silently in the door to signify his concern. Anson knew him, though he rarely looked up. And then it was that some keen and prying eye noted that the engagement ring had disappeared from Irena's finger.

The telephones rang off the hook.

Little Johnnes did mend, the blue cast of his flesh cleared, and his smothering spells lessened in frequency. Irena was to remember that, as the both of them bent over him one day, the infant opened his eyes, and so far as a ten-day-old can smile, he did.

"I see brown eyes!" Anson said, and then he burst into tears, pressing the tiny body to him. "My baby."

Irena and Anson had embraced. They were to recall with-out even speaking of it in their sometimes meetings in years to come. When this happened they wept again, the tears perhaps for what might have been.

The Victorians won out. The father-in-law did put his foot down, and Irena submitted again. He had sacrificed one daughter to Anson Winters and would not provide another. The diamond engagement ring presently returned to Irena's finger, although the marriage did not take place for several years. And Anson was not known to have looked at another woman. On this subject, the telephones operating in this wide community—such a relief and human satisfaction to isolated houses—had only questions, no confirmed answers. Where facts are missing, speculation takes over.

During the two weeks of Little Johnnes's crisis, the three-bed lying-in hospital had a number of visitors. Though the Winters generations kept largely to themselves, as did others of the large family conclaves of the region, they still carried on business relations, if few social ones. They held joint stock in enterprises, loaned workers or even cowboys in emergencies, bought from and sold to each other, and sometimes met in courthouses to iron out disputes not amenable to other solutions. In the matters of illness and death, in light of their own vulnerability, they were as one.

Visitors usually paused at the door and went no farther. Anson would raise his head for an instant, face deep in misery, and nod. The shade was drawn to keep light from the infant's eyes, the room dusky and always smelling of camphor. Irena would usually be there, and it was she who would rise, go to the door, and stepping beyond it, give what medical report there was to be offered.

As it happened, Irena was not present the time Lurie tried to visit. To make this call took some preparation, as well as courage and determination. Lurie lived with her sister and brother-in-law in a town twenty miles distant, and she only got to attend Melba's funeral because her brother-in-law had agreed with reluctance to drive her there. In his view as well as that of her sister, Velvet, it was hardly comely, as the families had never had business or social dealings. The single encounter between them had been years before when her father, as circuit judge, had presided over a case in court that went against the Winters claim, resulting in an expensive fence miles in length being built between the Bent Y Ranch and the neighbor to the north. It produced a long coolness between the families. Big Jack Winters had never claimed he was wronged. The case was moot. It could have gone either way. The injury was losing it.

The day after Melba's funeral, Lurie had bought an automobile—the Overland—to the alarm of her brother-in-law. This was an unheard of thing for a female to do. Nobody knew any woman who owned a car. But Lurie was determined to visit the hospital to see Anson and to view his child. She had been thinking of Anson since she was twelve years old, and she wasn't about to stop now. Velvet alone knew her sister's well-kept secret and couldn't find it within herself to wholly disapprove. And Velvet could keep a secret. The telephone wires were not to hum with this information for years to come.

Lurie could well afford to buy an automobile or anything else she might want. Her father, upon the death of his wife, having reached retirement age and the end of his last term in the same year, had gone to live with her elder brother, a cotton broker, in Waco. He had settled on his three children a substantial part of his estate, rental properties in the town and income from one third of the shares in a ranch in the Panhandle. The income was pooled and divided equally on an annual basis.

Lurie could already drive, having been allowed by her father to take the wheel on country roads when a girl. She never ditched the car, but, as her father complained, if there was a rock in the road, she managed to run over it. She became so adept she was allowed to drive the family on Sunday outings, even in passing through the town, which was as much a scandal as a female riding astride a horse in public instead of sidesaddle. Yet Lurie was far from being a tomboy. She was given to sewing her own clothes, when she might have had them done, and to decorating her summer hats with cloth flowers of the day. She practiced the art of crocheting, tatting, and knitting. Embroidered blouses were the work of her own fingers. But she was tough.

So Lurie drove to see Anson and his baby. As she steered up the street, she wondered if Anson would remember that day when she had been twelve and he had been seventeen, standing at the high fence between the elementary school and the high school, and she had first told him she loved him.

Lurie was never to recall the actual moment she noticed him for the first time. The bonding to him in her imagination had built gradually as she stood at the fence with other grade-school girls to watch the high school baseball team practice. Anson commanded third base and often ran within yards to retrieve a ball or catch a wild throw. She had on several occasions stayed on a few minutes after the other girls had left, and in time the chance to meet him came. A ball was batted the long way to the fence and lodged beneath the wire at her feet. Running for it, then stooping to retrieve it, Anson noticed her eyes upon him. He faced her and said, "You're a good backstop," and then Lurie was emboldened. "I love you," she said, as if it might be her last chance.

Anson raised up, ball in hand, and there was a smile of both pleasure and surprise on his face. "Ah," he said, "go play with your dolls." He had spoken it good-naturedly.

"You are my doll," she said.

The ball fell out of Anson's glove. He picked it up. He blushed. Lurie never forgot that.

"Little girl, what's your name?" he asked. He would have placed her by her surname, the circuit judge being her father.

She told him, and he ran back to his base. Once there, he turned around and faced her again and stared. And this was the last direct look between them until she stood in the door of the room in the hospital where the child lay. She was now seventeen, and he was twenty-two.

Lurie stood a full moment upon the doorsill before Anson, whose eyes were full of the sleeping infant, chanced to look up. Other than the child, he was alone.

He looked at her as if startled. And then she hurried from the room, not knowing what else to do, not even understanding why she had come. She had not even looked upon the child's face.

LURIE DID NOT LOOK upon Little Johnnes's face until six years later as he lay in his casket. She had been in Waco when her sister called to tell her, and she had driven through the night to be present at the funeral.

But Anson did not attend this funeral either. Hearsay had it that he lay in the hospital bed where his child had died, heavily sedated. Others had it that when Little Johnnes died Anson grabbed him up and tried to run out of the building and had to be restrained. It was also current that Anson had gone stark, raving mad.

Irena and her husband were not there either, as they were vacationing in Corpus Christi and did not receive word.

The telephone wires hummed.

None of the tales about Anson were true. He had not gone crazy. He was not drugged to forget his child's death. He had not tried to run away with the boy's body. In truth, Anson did lie on the child's bed, with Bronson holding his hand. His mother had sat there, too, stroking his head until it was time for her to depart for the funeral. Later she said, "Of all my children and grandchildren, I suppose I loved him the most because I worried about him the most."

Lurie told me that Little Johnnes lay pale and thin in his casket, seeming not flesh of this earth. He was a porcelain figurine, a whited sculpture. To view his face was to search for evidence of his parentage, and she recognized characteristics of both Anson and Melba. Anson was there in the shape of the head, the cheekbones, the chin; Melba was more elusively mirrored in the child's countenance, defying description. The light brown hair haloing his face was unmistakably the gift of Melba. The absence of Anson from the funeral had been large in the minds of the audience, as confidences were shared, whispered, ear to ear. Lurie overheard some of them: "Anson is out of his mind." "They've had to knock him out with laudanum." "He's strapped to a bed."

The rest of the Winters clan was there, save the absent daughter too distant to make the journey in time and Bronson, who had stayed by Anson's bedside. The menfolk presented a solemn attitude; the womenfolk wept silently. They did not cry, it was assumed, so much for the child who was now beyond pain and whose future had been cloudy. Instead, they wept for Anson, who had suffered from the child's suffering, who was in physical touch with him almost every moment from birth, who had kept him alive with his will and breath for six years.

The child was laid in the ground beside the marble slab of his mother, who had been the first of the Texas Winters family to die and thus the first one in this graveyard, which had been chosen because it was the closest one to the ranch.

At the Beech Ledge Cemetery, the only audible grief heard came from Ellafronia Cauldwell, who had been in the family's employ for two years, first as housekeeper and cook's helper, and was now referred to as "Papa's slave" by Anson, Jack, and Bronson. Her sole duty had evolved into the care and feeding and cajoling of Big Jack. The sons held their father in awe and treated their mother with kindly tolerance, as their difference in age had weakened the bonding that originally existed.

Ellafronia Cauldwell—Ella—had come out from Georgia in the vicinity of Macon, where the most pronounced and beautiful of Southern speech is cultivated, to visit the family of an aunt. She had stayed on, winding up at the big house when, as gossip had it, her aunt grew jealous of the marked attentions of her husband to the newcomer. According to Lurie, Ella was not pretty. Good-looking might have been the word used by teasing cowboys. Everybody liked her. Her patience with Big Jack as he grew petulant was phenomenal. When any disagreement arose over the operation of the Bent Y, Ella could be counted on to mollify him. So Ella's sniffing, heard above the murmurs of the brief graveside ceremony, came to Lurie's attention. Ella was Anson's age, trapped in a territory where most men were married by nineteen, almost certainly by twenty-one. She had verged on spinsterhood in Georgia and passed it in Texas. No other unmarried woman came in contact more frequently with Anson.

At the Beech Ledge Cemetery, there were no beech trees and never had been. Nor was there any ledge. The ground was flat as a table. The original settler of the land thereabout had named it for the one where his parents were buried. Several of his children had died in infancy, along with two wives, and eventually he had been interred there himself. There were trees shading the graves—great, evergreen live oaks, which had preceded the founding of the cemetery and which gummed the grave stones at their almost secret blooming in spring and showered the ground with spent leaves throughout the year.

Before the lowering of the casket into the grave, the Winters family departed, as was the custom. Others, who had arrived by buggy, carriage, and horseback, lingered. Only two automobiles had tracked the half-wilderness road to the isolated cemetery: the Winterses' Hudson and Lurie's Overland.

Lurie's vehicle drew attention, particularly that of the women. Yet the envy or the disapproval was masked. There was many an "Oh!" and "Ah!" The wife of the preacher cried out, "How cunning!" Whatever that meant. But Lurie was not attending these social nuances concerning the car, which spoke more than was actually put into words.

Lurie was struck by a symbolic act following the end of the preacher's exhortation when he had said "Ashes to ashes, dust to dust" and dropped a rose into the open grave. Jack had stepped forward and more pitched than dropped a small object into the hole. It happened unexpectedly, and the viewers who usually missed nothing construed it to be another blossom. It made a small thud as it struck the casket, or so Lurie believed. There was no further mention of this act among them. Later she was to ask Jack directly, and he said it was the gold safety pin their sister had sent to the shower party given Melba after they had announced their forthcoming wedding. It had been Little Johnnes's first toy. Pinned to his collar, it served as a teether and had been latched to his rompers or shirt pocket all his life, as it had remained a wonder to him.

Lurie lingered among the graves, as anxious as any for details not known to her. Since the age of twelve she had filed away in her mind every scrap of information concerning the Winters family. Here, under the live oaks, she listened. The shaking of hands, the greetings, the comments on the dead child. Talk of the father took place, as it would have at any funeral.

Lurie learned little, for they knew little.

"Anson could diaper a baby as good as any woman, and as quick."

"I was in a grocery store once, and in came Anson Winters, and he bought something, and he stuck his hand in a pocket to get some change, and out came a bunch of safety pins along with the money. Sad and sort of funny, too."

"Reckon he washed the diapers?"

"Naw, he has help at that cotton farm. At the ranch, too. Women to help."

"Yes, women. Mexican women, at the farm."

"Hmm! I wonder!"

"By the time the child was two, he didn't need help. Didn't want help. He was mostly holding on to the child, or the child holding on to him, all hours of day and night. They were one."

"Anson done a job my husband wouldn't've undertook. I praise him for it."

"With his wife gone, his child dead, what now?"

"Some floozy will hook him."

"Wouldn't you like to be the one?"

Smothered laughter.

News of what did follow in the months ahead, or in the next two and a half years ahead, was hard to come by. But even in such a place, where farms and ranches were miles apart—sometimes counties apart—there was always somebody who knew somebody who had gleaned a grain of it and passed it along, however flawed in passage.

The telephone system was subject to frequent breakdowns, was given occasionally to unaccountable roarings the human voice could barely surmount. Should you ring up past eight o'clock in the evening, you got an operator out of bed (since the switchboards were located in homes), and not always grudgingly, as the pleasure of listening in made up for the disturbance. If you called a party, you could be assured of a dozen or so listeners. Gossip pieces together like scraps of a quilt.

Lurie refused to listen in, but her sister was not so abstemious.

More than a year and a half passed before Velvet collected the bits and pieces about Anson's first visit to the grave of his son. During this time, Lurie had lived at the home of her parents, who had retired to a house next door to her brother, the cotton broker. She was leaning toward spinsterhood, to the concern of her brother. Her brother's wife saw to it that her social life was not lacking, that eligible unmarried men and a widower or two knew of her existence, were invited to dinner, and to Sunday evening socials. Suitors are not hard to find when the girl has property, along with gentle rearing and beauty. One of them might have made his way into her heart had it not been for her memory of Anson. He stood between her and any other man. Moreover, Irena had married at last. And there was no news of any matching up with Ellafronia, as handy as that might have been.

Eventually, talk of Anson's being crazy died out, so talk of him petered out, too. Lurie was suddenly deprived of any certain knowledge of Anson. For some six months he had lived at the ranch, and then the word was he had returned to Chinaberry, making himself busy with the production of cotton. As therapy, it was assumed. The tales had it that he actually worked occasionally in the fields and got his hands dirty. All three of the Winters brothers had long since given up cowpunching. Hired hands herded the cattle.

To occupy the time, Lurie enrolled in practical nursing classes at an Amarillo (pronounced Amirilla in those parts) hospital. Her bent was toward the illnesses and care of children. The courses were general—physiology and nutrition. Next, as much a prank as anything else, she took a charm class taught evenings at a beauty parlor. Above all else she learned about "hair culture," which was the care and feeding of the female scalp, as well as the many ways she could "put up" her shoulder-length hair, which was to me as corn silk in sunlight. Her sister-in-law had put her up to it, to enhance still further her opportunities toward matrimony.

The time was hard to endure, the distance impossible to bear. So she went home to her sister. She would have rented a house or lived in one she owned, but it was not socially feasible for a lady of her age to live alone. Nor was it considered safe. For a widow perhaps, but not for an unmarried twenty-seven-year-old. It had been fifteen years since she had stood at the schoolyard fence and told Anson, "You are my doll."

CHAPTER six

Towerhouse

LURIE AND ANSON had dressed me like a toy cowboy. On my head was a small Stetson, on my feet, cowboy boots with sharp toes. My pants were store-bought, but the shirt was one Lurie had cut out and sewed to match Anson's.

The occasion for my outfit was a trip out to the ranch, where Anson was taking us that Sunday. When a job required his presence there most of the week, he usually spurned returning on Saturday or Sunday. Two months from now, during shipping season, he would have to be there seven days a week, so he cherished his weekends at home. But he wanted me to meet his parents, so he and Lurie had agreed to have Sunday supper at the main house.

Anson had been telling me about the ranch, the cows, the horses and their foals, the feeder calves, the cowboys. About the herd that grazed for miles and miles on a free range. We would see cowboys in action. He told me about Pop Cod. He talked somewhat of cotton farming, but there was nothing I needed to be told, as I had been in on the ground floor of the subject since birth.

"Is there a towerhouse with electric lights?" I asked.

"Naw, naw," Anson said, and he laughed a little, cutting his eyes to Lurie, who smiled. "The house is just called the Towerhouse. On account of the man who built it."

I was to learn of this man later, along with much more information.

I had heard many tales about everyone who lived at the ranch and was anxious to experience meeting them. There were Anson's parents, plus his brother Jack and Jack's three sons, who were always referred to as "the three Little Jacks." Also Ellafronia Cauldwell, Bronson, the cook with the dim-witted son, the cowboys, and the helpers who might drop in at any hour and be fed at their appointed table.

Despite being told ahead of time that there was no tower at Towerhouse, unless I wanted to count the silo, I expected one as we turned down the drive. The Winters homestead sat atop a rise of ground that could be seen by keen eyes a full mile's distance, the spread of land about it as flat as a beaver's tail and planted in corn and millet. Still, this was no "big hill," as Anson said, although I suppose it could be considered as such in a place as flat as East Texas. We had encountered no cotton since crossing into Robertson County. The distance from the main road to the house was accounted at two miles.

We stepped out of the car, and the sun hazed like a copper skillet. A light breeze stirred, as always.

We were met at the yard gate by Anson's mother, Jack, and the three Little Jacks. They stared at me and my toy cowboy getup. They were dressed well but not fancy.

We were chided for being late. Dinner awaited on the table, and after embracing her son and Lurie, Anson's mother—whom I had been instructed to call "Grandma"—put her hands on my shoulders and studied me lovingly. "So here's the boy I've been hearing brags about," she exclaimed. "So this is the one." She gave me a hug and a kiss and pushed me back, appraising me again. I resisted wiping away the damp spot on my cheek, which I wouldn't have hesitated to do back in Alabama.

Jack caught hold of my hand, and one of the Little Jacks pulled his father's hand loose and substituted his own. Everybody laughed at this.

"We all know who he reminds us of," Grandma said. I didn't understand.

Anson picked me up, which pained me, as it usually did when we were in front of others. Lurie must have sensed my discomfort, because she touched his arm lightly. "Let him walk along with the three Little Jacks," she said. So he did.

The moment we stepped onto the porch, I heard the grind of the ice cream freezer and smelled the mixed aromas familiar to Sunday dinners back home: fried chicken, dumplings, cured ham, gravy, smoking biscuits, green beans, potatoes, apple pie, pound cake, pickles, jams, and jellies. And most to my liking, there was the scent of sweet potato pie.

Having washed our hands at the water shelf on the back porch, we were led directly to the dining room and seated. Already at the table was Big Jack. He patted me on the head and said, "Good boy." After that, he didn't more than glance my way. It turned out he had not been told about me. Later, I heard Anson whisper to Lurie, "No use telling Papa anything he might not be able to handle."

I sat between Lurie and Anson. Anson served my plate, seeing to it that I got something of everything. Jack's wife, Nora, sat on one side of Grandpa, with Jack on the other. But wedged against Grandpa's chair was "Jacky Boy," the middle of the three boys, who was Grandpa's favorite. Grandpa ate little but insisted on Jacky Boy's stuffing himself. Ellafronia flew up and down from her seat, to the kitchen and back with further dishes, checking to see that Grandpa actually ate something, which he wouldn't unless urged.

"You need to eat a bit more now, Big Jack," Ellafronia said in her tender way.

"Just to smell dinner fills me up," he replied.

The cook came to the dining room door and looked us over. The grinding of the ice cream cooler stopped a moment, and then the cook's son peeped in, too. He was nineteen, but he had the mind of a three-year-old. I had heard Anson talking about him before, his voice full of pity.

I ate mostly sweet potato pie, yet no one questioned my choice. And then there was the ice cream, a heaping mound in a bowl when I had little room left. And the cook appeared with a giant bowl of charlotte russe, which he called the "piece de resistance." As badly as I wanted to partake, there was no room left in my belly.

There was an empty chair saved for Ernest Roughton. Work hands didn't usually eat with the family. They had their meals with any cowpuncher who showed up at a table on the screened porch. But since I was to be at dinner, he had been invited. Was his absence due to the class distinction he wasn't subject to during other times? Perhaps he didn't feel right in breaking bread with them only because I was to be there.

He did come later, ate on the porch, and managed to get me aside. Not an easy matter with Anson present, and I was keenly aware of Anson's monitoring me while I talked to Ernest.

Anson's explanation for Ernest's absence at the table was that horses and calves and pigs and milk cows don't know Sunday from any other day of the week. They have to be fed, watered, catered to, or milked or curried or combed. Fence posts don't wait until Monday to be uprooted. A horse is as apt to throw a shoe on the Sabbath as on any other day of the week. Flies don't delay until a second day of the week to blow a heifer's laceration, so you have to be quick with the tar even when church beckons. Anson had read my dejection over missing Ernest. I was counting on seeing him. My homesickness was sometimes worn like a cloak and sometimes glimmered at the back of my mind, but it was always there, and I hardly ever saw Ernest or the Knuckleheads lately. I needed Alabama voices.

After the long dinner—it was fully two o'clock and the hottest part of one of the hottest days we'd had thus far—Jack and the three Little Jacks returned to their nearby house. When they left I heard Jack say they were going early so Grandpa could "try the little one on for size," talking about me.

Once they had gone, there came my nap time. My eyelids were dropping when Anson caught me up and deposited me on a cot on a shady side porch. Naps were especially important on this day, as we had all grown up with the spoken notion that "Everybody with gumption takes a nap on Sunday." Anson stayed a moment to pull off my boots and loosen my collar, to fan me with his hat until I slept, and he was back when I waked with a pan of water and towel to freshen my hands and face.

By the time I arose, Grandpa had been told something about me. I was placed on his lap, which seemed large enough for several my size. His great hands were covered with spots. The flesh of his face had been so long tanned by wind and sun that it seemed like leather. He was in his eighties.

"You like Texas?" he asked.

"Yessir," I said.

"Better than Alabama?"

"Nawsir."

Big Jack grinned. "Well, he's honest." Then he said to me, "I was born in East Tennessee and raised in West Tennessee. Learned to stay off the skid road in the logging woods of British Columbia." He furrowed his brow and gave me a warning, having noted Anson's penchant for carrying me: "Walk on your own legs. Don't let that son of mine make a puppy dog of you."

Grandma chimed in, defending Anson: "I want Anson to do what in his heart he needs to do. This boy is good for him."

"I raised Anson, and I know him from his ears to his toenails," the old man said, his wit and wisdom coming through. "Come stay here at the Towerhouse with us and you'll fare better. We'll neglect you a little."

Ellafronia Cauldwell came into the room to say Ernest was having his dinner on the screened porch and would like to see me. Anson started to follow, but Lurie stayed him.

"Hey-o, Skybo!" Ernest greeted me with much cheer.

Seeing Ernest aroused an emotion I hadn't expected. Before taking the trip west, I had never exchanged words with him. The poolroom he managed back home was off limits to youth, besides being rated a den of iniquity where men smoked cigars, spoke cuss words, gambled with cards, and probably drank liquor. A fifth-grade classmate reported passing Ernest's place once and heard somebody, perhaps having miscued a ball, shout "Damn!" I always glanced in furtively on the way to school and never saw anything untoward. This was my father's one vice, shooting pool. He was said to be a "mean" player.

When I saw Ernest, the homesickness that had been packed away and unacknowledged inside of me arose like a ball in my throat, choking me. I could only manage a "Hey." There came instantly to mind a stanza of the Alabama state song we used to sing in school, not even thinking about the words we knew so well by heart:

Broad the Stream whose name thou bearest;
Grand thy Bigbee rolls along;
Fair thy Coosa-Tallapoosa

Bold thy warrior, dark and strong.
Goodlier than the land that Moses
Climbed lone Nebo's mount to see,
Alabama, Alabama,
We will aye be true to thee!

Ernest spoke up: "Aye, they're fattening you! How many pounds have you picked up?"

"Three," I said. Other words were like a foam in my mouth. I wanted to ask when we were going home, and I could not. I wanted to go home, and yet I didn't want to leave Anson and Lurie—particularly Lurie. It was a paradox too great for a thirteen-year-old to surmount.

It turned out that my mother was writing me weekly, Ernest said, and my father had had an exchange of a couple of letters with Ernest, checking on me.

Papa had wanted to know when Ernest was bringing me home, insisting on a date. Ernest had replied that he was back dealing with horses, back to the satisfactory days when he worked at a livery stable. He wanted to consolidate himself in his new job before asking for leave for a quick trip. But he would return. Moreover, if anything, I was being too well looked after, he told my father. He assured my parents that I was the cynosure of all eyes in the Anson Winters family and that my every step was trailed by the old Indian, who never allowed me out of his sight.

The second letter from my father reminded Ernest that Chambers County schools opened in middle September. He didn't want me to miss a day. Ernest's reply was news to me. The Winterses would start me in a Robertson County school at about the same time. And he reminded my father of his several years of residing in Texas, of his longtime regret that he hadn't remained.

Much later I was to read that letter:

You wanted this son of yours to experience Texas, the reason you wanted him to come with me. He's *experiencing* it in a fashion you'd never guess. Let him have it for a few more weeks. The only trouble will be, as it was with you, he'll never be plumb happy in Alabama if he stays in Texas too long. I'll try to get him returned before that happens.

This was enough to mollify my father for a while. My mother was not happy about this, though. With all the children she already had to look after, and with more to come, she wanted them all where she could see them.

Anson was chafing to leave when I returned to the living room, and during my absence Grandma was trying to convince him to let me stay overnight. As I walked in she was saying, "You'll be back here tomorrow anyway. Let him stay so I can talk to him, get better acquainted. He hasn't seen the colts, seen the place, looked around."

I just wanted to see the cowboys.

Grandma was hard to deny. Anson had denied her only once, when she had insisted on caring for Little Johnnes after the death of his mother. Anson believed he alone could keep the child alive. "Ah," she was to tell me, referring to the baby as "it," as people were apt to do. "How he strove with it, when its wind shut off! He'd work with it, pump its lungs up and down, thought he could keep it alive forever with his own breath. Break your heart to watch him."

Anson relented, and he and Lurie drove away. We watched the Overland for a long time, until it became a speck and vanished into the horizon. Then Grandma said, "He'll be back."

Ernest took me in hand. We visited the horses and their foals in the corral, the feeder calves, the tack room, where harnesses and saddles were hanging. I saw one cowpuncher ride in, pitch his saddle in the backseat of a Ford, put a finger to the brim of his worn hat when he saw me in my little Stetson and boots, and then he saluted, "Hey-o, cowboy."

Anson was to tell me this: "Cowhands think more of their saddles than they do of their wives. Think they'd leave them in the tack room? Some saddles are worth hundreds of dollars for all the silver filigree on them."

As we walked by the bunkhouse, we spied an ancient man propped in a chair on the porch. "That's old Pop Cod," Ernest whispered. This was the old cowboy I had heard so much about from Anson. "I'd introduce you, but he's had a sick spell. Just been out of bed a day or two."

We heard the Overland coming long before we could see it in the gathering dusk. Grandma had been right; Anson was coming back for me.

Anson strode up onto the porch and picked me up.

Grandma rose. "What's the matter?" she asked.

"We need him," Anson said.

CHAPTER *seven*

Magnolia grandiflora; Or, Anson and Lurie, Revisited

I WAS TO HEAR of Lurie and Anson's courtship on one of those late afternoons when we sat outside, awaiting Anson's return. A telephone message came through from Towerhouse to let us know that Anson would be late; he was dickering with a buyer for the feeder calves. As Lurie and I were bathed and dressed in our freshly laundered garments, there was nothing else to do but sit in the swing and keep waiting for him.

That day Lurie may have had her sunny hair done up in plaits, wrapped round her head, held in place by celluloid combs that bore tiny rhinestones. Or she may have had her hair in any of the other fashions she knew how to achieve, sometimes assisted by Angelica. One thing is sure: she smelled of violets. I was as scrubbed as she. Lurie would probably have rubbed some of Anson's Lucky Tiger tonic onto my hair, and if the Knuckleheads had seen me they would have clucked my ears and told me that I "stunk."

To whom else would Lurie have told of her courtship and marriage to Anson? Certainly not to Angelica and Rosetta, not to any of her own town acquaintances. Aside from her sister, I was likely the only person to ever hear the details.

After Little Johnnes died, there was, of course, plenty of hearsay about Anson: he had donned spurs and chaps and become a cowpuncher again; he was out of his head and shut up in a room; he was living at Chinaberry, managing the seventy-five acres of cotton, sometimes even taking a hand at the plow. This last had turned out to be true, as Lurie was to learn for herself.

On returning from the months spent in the households of her parents and brother—their houses stood side by side in Amarillo—she felt liberated enough to drive about in her Overland without female companions as chaperones. But not enough to live alone, in one of the houses that were now her own rental properties in town. Society allowed this privilege to widows only, as they were beyond the age of passion.

Before leaving Amarillo, she had written Anson a letter expressing sympathy for the death of his son, addressing it to the Bent Y Ranch, Bluewater, Texas. In the letter, she identified herself as the twelve-year-old fan who, years before, had backstopped a baseball thrown for him at the schoolyard fence. There was no reply.

On returning to her sister's home, she wrote another, repeating the greeting of sympathy and the reminder, on the assumption that the first letter had gone astray, not an unlikely happening in those days. This time she addressed it to Route 2, Clover Creek, Texas. The mail carrier furnished the address and assured its delivery. The result was silence.

Lurie was to discover both these letters, along with several others addressed in unmistakable female script, in a drawer, unopened, years later. None, including her own, bore a return address on the envelopes. She wasn't alone in being concerned about Anson's welfare and in seeking his attention.

There was only one other way to see Anson—to go to where he was. On the assumption that the rumor of his now living at Chinaberry was true, she began to drive past his farm two days a week, leaving the main highway south and taking the narrower lane of the mail route. Of this ruse she told no one, not even her sister. A two-day-a-week trip would go unnoticed.

As luck, coincidence, or whatever force decides such matters would have it, on her sixth trip her gamble was rewarded. Anson was plowing, breaking ground with a moldboard plow, in the same field with another plowman, Blunt the Indian. It seemed not something Anson would ordinarily be doing. And it wasn't. He had taken over for Blunt for a short turn at the plow to get a feel for the elasticity of the soil. It was April, when moisture content, the readiness for planting, is fed by "feel" up through the plow handles.

There was nothing else for it. As Lurie had bravely stated her case in the schoolyard years before, she parked the car on a grassy shoulder and walked across the broken ground to Anson. Blunt retreated to a distance out of hearing.

Anson stood holding the plow lines, motionless. He pulled off his straw hat, a sombrero, and wiped his forehead with a sleeve. As Lurie told it to me, she remembered everything. The butterflies in the sun. The bobwhites calling from the hedgerows. The wedding ring still on Anson's finger. His gray eyes looking puzzled.

They greeted each other. She expressed regrets at the loss of his child, and he seemed to have no words in reply. Then she asked, "Do you remember me?"

"Very well," he said. "You're the little girl who backstopped my baseball. And told me something."

"You remember that?"

"I do. And I remember another thing. Your hair—your beautiful hair."

Lurie was on the verge of tears, telling this part.

Regaining her car, she thought to herself to drive on past, wait until he had plowed out of sight, then turn around and drive back the way she had come. She wanted to leave the impression that her passing was accidental. When she came past she saw him still standing by the moldboard plow. He hadn't moved.

When she reached her sister's home and confessed to this transgression of good manners, Velvet told her she should now show some encouragement to the suitor her same age, who drove the long distance occasionally to see her. He had finished medical school and was doing his internship in New Braunfels. He was ideal in her sister's eyes: personable, a good raising, with a future. To Lurie, this man might have everything, but he was not Anson.

Three Sundays later, Anson arrived at Lurie's sister's home in middle afternoon. He would not come into the house or sit on the porch. "Passing by," he said, and he did sit a moment on a top step, talking with her brother-in-law.

The next Sunday he was back and was persuaded to sit on the porch. The next, he came riding a saddle horse and leading another. They went for a canter down the main street of the town and a half mile beyond until they approached a cemetery. He turned abruptly about, and they rode back. The following Saturday he came in a Stutz, and they rode for miles. She wrote to her suitor in New Braunfels and said she hoped they could remain friends.

"The telephone will be ringing," she told Anson. "People will talk."

Neither of them cared.

More than a year passed. He seemed to be making an adjustment in his mind to break free from a bond that held him. One Sunday, in July, he brought a magnolia blossom and pressed its twig into her hair. He had made many a comment on her hair, had taken to stroking it. He wanted her to wear it loose about her shoulders, but she felt that was for a younger person than her age. Yet, to please him, she did wear it long occasionally, tied with a ribbon. The first kiss from him was on the ear, with her hair pulled over his face.

On the day he brought the magnolia, he suddenly indicated the finger bearing a wedding ring and asked, "Would you ask me to pull this off?"

Lurie assured him she would not.

That constituted his proposal of marriage.

He said he had already made arrangements.

"For when?"

"Tomorrow, in the clerk's office." And, he added, "So the telephones will stop ringing."

Although he offered many endearments during his courtship, he had never said "I love you." She wondered if this would come later. Lurie was alert to every nuance. She noted that he called her "sweet heart"—two words, not "sweetheart."

"Does your family know about this?" Lurie found herself asking.

"No, we'll surprise them."

"How will they feel about it?"

"They'll be tickled," he said. "Especially Mama."

Then Lurie pressed, surprised at her courage. "Do you love me?"

"I need you," Anson said.

CHAPTER eight

The Breaking In

LOOKING BACK TO my time at Chinaberry, I can now understand that Lurie was both delighted and concerned by my unex-
pected appearance in their midst. Concerned that I could only be
temporary, that Anson's involvement with another child might
be too great, only to suffer loss again. She was to tell me in due
course, and at a moment of bitterness, that we were both substitutes. She was the substitute for his dead wife and maybe even
for Irena, the sister whom he would have married. I was the
substitute for the lost son, of course, the son who had been more
than an offspring, who for six years had been pressed against
him, or, when he needed both hands for a task, who would circle
arms about his neck, to whom Anson would say, softly, "Hold on,
baby. Hold on."

For a long while she had believed that when he said "Hold on"
in the middle of the night he was asleep. She learned from his
reaching for what was not there and from his sitting up that it
wasn't a dream. As often as twice a week, he rose up in the night
and slipped on his moccasins and walked outside. The act of
putting on the moccasins proved he was not sleepwalking. One
moonlit night, from the doorway, she watched him in his noctur-
nal wandering, around the house, out to the fields, down the lane
to the mailbox. Once he was gone fully two hours, having climbed
on his saddle horse bareback and ridden off into the pasture.

When I came to live at Chinaberry, he was to go into the night only once more. But he did rise up in bed the second night of my stay and listen. I was asleep on the trundle bed in the adjoining room, where he had sat beside me until I slept, told me good night three times, and finally said over and over like an incantation, "Sleepy sleep, sleepy sleep." At home I slept alone, and here I would have succumbed to slumber quicker had he not been there.

That night Anson had risen up in bed, and when Lurie brought herself to inquire, "What's the matter?" he had said, "I can't hear the baby breathing."

"Go to him," Lurie said, and he did.

Unknown to me, he placed a hand on my chest until he was satisfied my breathing was regular.

The next day my trundle bed was rolled into their bedroom, where they could keep better tabs. The room was not especially large, with their brass bed in one corner and my trundle in the other. I had only to call, should I need him, he said.

It came about that I was to address Anson as "Dad-o." This was what the three Little Jacks called their father. I had dismissed "Papa," which had been suggested. I had a papa back in Alabama. There could be no other.

I remember the first time I called him this, on a morning when he brought the pan of water and the washcloth for the morning's ablutions. This had been a busy week, and we had seen little of him. As I was just coming to consciousness from sleep, lingering somewhere in a dream world, Anson had leaned over me and asked, "Do you know me?"

I said, apparently without hesitation, "You're Dad-o." This had pleased him to no end, according to Lurie. As I had come to represent a phantom Johnnes, Anson had become a father image, a stay against the homesickness that often haunted me. To my mind he even began to look like Papa: the sandy hair, the gray-blue eyes, the same set of jaw. When I sat on Anson's lap, I could imagine I was sitting on my father's, which I never recollect doing. My brother, who had taken my short-lived place as the baby, was in my own Papa's lap, in a place rightly mine. My mother and sisters nuzzled at my little brother, and I was assigned to adulthood at age two. I bore no resentment outwardly, but it must have been there inwardly. A neglected child was being belatedly rewarded. Given time, nature asserts itself, exacts its revenge.

In the case of Lurie, she never took on a maternal image in my mind. Beautiful, warmhearted, she took me into her confidence. I was kept fairly contented at Chinaberry because of her presence and ministrations. When she pressed me to her bosom, something stirred in my heart. It was that biologically unexplainable term—love.

I might even have grown a smidgen jealous of Anson. One day he came home from work and embraced me only hurriedly, moving on to her, whom he did not release from his embrace.

"Wait," she said. "Later."

But he wasn't about to let go of her. "I can't wait," he said. Then he turned to me and said, "Go see what Blunt's doing."

What did a thirteen-year-old in those days know? Not much. But I half-knew what they were about to do. I ran off the porch to the rear of the house, where Blunt sat working with his awls on a harness. Blunt saw my dolesome face, so he dropped his handwork, picked up a baseball nearby, and threw it to me. I let it fall. Blunt made no further effort.

When Anson came out to me, I was swelled up with resentment.

"Look at me," he pleaded, but I wouldn't.

He pressed me against him, nibbled on my chin and my ears. "Cry a little, it will help," he said.

I wanted to, but I couldn't.

Here was the politics of rejection. He struck a bargain with me, and he kept it. He promised if I would forgive him he'd never send me away again. And—the bonus—he would stay with me that night, all night. I submitted, and then the tears came. Homesickness overwhelmed me. I might have asked him then, while he was vulnerable, about this big thing that was in my head.

But I waited until night, while we were in bed, after the mantle lamp had been blown out. When he asked me, as he did daily, "Are you still my baby boy?" I did not answer "Yes, sir," as I had been coached by Lurie to do. Not right away. I hesitated, finally saying, "Uh huh," which had a degree of disrespect in it. Then, I said, "Dad-o?"

"Yes, baby," he said. In speaking to Lurie, Anson referred to me as "the baby." To others he referred to me as "the little man" or "the boy."

I couldn't get the words clear of my teeth. While I knew he would do anything within reason for me, my request couldn't come forth for a moment. Finally, it came out with a rush, and to fortify my request, I locked my arms about his neck. "Take me home," I said, and saying it came hard. What I had already envisaged was that he and Lurie would drive me back to Alabama in the Hudson, and after a few days they'd decide to stay there with me and my family. Either that or my family would go back with us. As my parents had agreed to almost everything I had proposed in my life, including the unprecedented trip to Texas of a thirteen-year-old in company of a friend, I could not imagine they'd insist that I stay in Alabama. Anson had only to ask, I thought. Nobody ever denied Anson anything.

Anson did not reply for a long while. He alternately pushed me away from him and embraced me tighter. Pressing his mouth to my ear, he said, "My little man . . . my little Anson . . . my baby boy—you're already home."

FROM THE NIGHT when Anson had snipped off my hanging toenail, my feet had been the subject of inspection at bedtime. Nothing was going to make them lose their brownness. From May first until first frost, no country boy in Alabama wore shoes except on Church Sunday, which was one day out of the month.

My skin was also always attended to by Lurie, using both the arts of medicine and her beauty training. My ankles and heels were rubbed with cold cream, as were my elbows. The red spots caused by mosquitoes were touched with turpentine.

Then there were my haircuts. Anson always stood by to advise, to make sure it was cut to his specification, to the pattern of his own. Lurie was an expert. After cutting my hair, they combed it this way and that. He combed it one way, she combed it another. They fussed a little, as much of a disagreement as they were ever to have, except for when they argued about how little I ate, or some other little thing.

What I wanted to eat most of all were cornflakes, floating around in sweet milk, heavily sweetened. They wanted me to eat eggs and biscuits and bacon. At supper Anson piled meat and potatoes and beans onto my plate. I would eat a portion, then look at the pie or cake. To glance at it was to be served a slice by Lurie. Anson thought I should eat more of the "solid stuff," and he would poke additional bites with a fork into my mouth. Lurie, from her limited hospital experience, believed that I should not be coerced into eating more than I wanted. Given time, I would adjust, she said. I always drank buttermilk, shunning the evil-smelling and bad-tasting drinking water.

My presence brought about two changes, one overnight, the other within a couple of weeks. The outdoor privy, used by Angelica and Rosetta, and most anyone else not a member of the family, was the one I used out of necessity. There were three holes, one child-size. The bathroom in the house was down a long hall from our bedroom, pitch dark at night. It was so far a distance that a chamber pot was placed at the foot of my bed, one I never found cause to use. My natural functions took place during daylight hours. In this bathroom, the commode was too high from the floor, too large at the opening. I couldn't reach the pull-chain to flush. Blunt had the remedy. A board, with a hole to fit my anatomy, was fashioned so I wouldn't fall in. It could be readily set onto the commode. A box platform was constructed to support my feet. A boot string lengthened the pull-chain.

Our noon meal was treated as a picnic. Angelica and Rosetta served Lurie and me sandwiches—chicken, turkey, peanut butter, or pimento. And iced tea spiked with lemon flavoring, sweetened for me. Four tablespoons of sugar almost killed the curious taste of the water. Not quite, though. Our favorite dining spot was the double wooden swing under the chinaberry trees, where those on the swing had to face each other for balance.

After one such leisurely lunch, Lurie carted me to the doctor. She had decided I needed to go because Anson had taken to doing asthma exercises on me every morning. He made a game of it, stretching me out flat on the carpet, placing a hand on either side of my chest, raising me up and pressing down, pumping air into my lungs. I didn't understand the need for it, but somehow I knew that it was more for Anson than for me. On several occasions, while setting up the breathing routine, he whispered, "I had a little boy once."

So Lurie decided that my lungs should be checked, to put Anson's mind at ease. Undoubtedly the doctor knew Anson's case well, and he reported accordingly. Thumping my chest, listening with a stethoscope front and back, he summoned the diagnosis. "Best set of bellows you'll ever find. You could hire him out to a blacksmith," the doctor said. "He'll be breathing when the rest of us are dead."

We were to meet again, the doctor and I.

Next, a dentist had a look at my teeth. "There's a couple wisdom teeth aiming to come through or try to," he said, peering in at my mouth again. "He might need me then."

I was never to require his services.

Anson was breaking me in.

If he had not gone for the day when I awaked, it was he who brought the glass of freestone water with a lump of ice in it, along with the pan of warm water with a washrag to clear the "sand" from my eyes and freshen my face and hands. Chinaberry had recently acquired a portable water fountain, replete with a five-gallon glass jug of freestone water, half-housed in an insulated box kept filled with ice. One had only to turn a tap to fill a glass. It was almost as good as Alabama water. After my ice water and my face washing, Anson picked me up, carrying me as easily as a pillow to the bathroom. The same exchange always occurred. "Heavy," I said. "As chicken feathers," he said.

I still was not used to Anson's need to pick me up, to carry me in his arms as he had his son for six years. I came gradually to not mind, but it was awkward. Then I was taking all my cues from Lurie. She approved, but she must have harbored fears about what appeared to be an emotional bondage. I'd glance round at her, she would nod, and up my arms would go for me to be taken up. We took trips to the barn to admire the saddle horses' beauty, to the cotton house, to the edge of the fields where the cotton picking progressed, out to the mailbox, which was a good quarter-mile walk, one way. I would have already "robbed" the mailbox, looking for a letter from Alabama. One generally arrived on Saturday or Monday, from my mother. Gloomy were my weekend prospects if Saturday was not the day.

ERNEST CAME OVER to Chinaberry in his Model T to check on me every week or so.

One morning I was hidden behind one of the swaying chinaberry trees when they all stood together, looking out across the flat plains. No one knew I was there.

"You are spoiling that boy rotten," Ernest said.

"What I'm trying to do," Anson admitted. "I want him to like me. When he does go back to Alabama, I want him to be so dissatisfied they'll send him back."

"I don't know," Ernest said. "He's the first boy after five daughters. You can guess how a man feels about his first son after five tries."

Turning away, Anson said, "I don't want to hear it. Something may work out."

"I doubt it," Ernest said, not to raise false hopes.

"The boy's father let him come off with you. Proves he can get by without him. He's got two younger brothers, he says."

"You don't understand his pappy. I know him to the bone," Ernest said. "He let this boy come in his stead. He homesteaded himself out here in the 1890s, out near Killeen, and never got Texas out of his mind. This minute he's wearing a Stetson and cowboy boots. Visiting back in Alabama, the family lost a child, and the mother decided against returning to Texas."

Anson had heard this before from me, and he also knew of my father's profession. "We could use a veterinarian," he said. "Give him about all the work he could handle at our ranch alone, and there's the Bolton ranch north of us, twice the size of the Bent Y. They'd give more than he could do."

"That's an idea," Ernest said.

I could have told them with the little wisdom a thirteen-year-old had gathered that this couldn't happen. Mama had told us often of her promise to my sister, before she died of scarlet fever at age five, that she would never leave her. She was as committed to staying near the Rock Springs graveyard as Anson Winters was tied to the Beech Ledge Cemetery.

Still, Anson was determined to have me.

Anson and Lurie had been married almost three years. I put my face against the chinaberry tree, wondering why they had no child of their own.

CHAPTER nine

Oxyuris vermicularis

THE TEMPERATURE HOVERED at ninety degrees during most of August, often rising to ninety-eight, and more than occasionally past one hundred for the hottest part of the day. We took many cooling baths. Anson and I favored the shower in the washhouse while Lurie soaked in the bathtub. Understanding the curious modesty of boys my age, Anson never entered the washhouse while I was there, and we stood together under the shower only when wearing our undershorts or the truncated bathing suits.

Saturday afternoons I went with Anson to cool off at the horse pond, the smallest of the three ponds formed by a windmill pump, assisted by a gasoline engine when the wind failed to keep the five-hundred-gallon tank filled. Our bathing suits were made by Lurie, fashioned from a store-bought pattern, which decreed that only our heads, arms, and legs below the knee were showing. Later Lurie came upon a picture of folks on a California beach, which caused her to cut off the tops, freeing our arms and chests.

Fans were everywhere at Chinaberry. At the foot of the beds, on bureaus, on the sideboard. Palmetto fans. Angelica and Rosetta fanned themselves with one hand and cooked with the other when the tasks allowed. In the swing, after supper, while dust settled about, I sat between Anson and Lurie. Anson's left arm embraced Lurie's shoulders while his right hand was engaged in keeping us fanned during the momentary lulls in the fairly constant breeze. Anson had explained that the wind caused the difference in temperature of earth and the air above it, the pause coming about when the temperature of both reached equality. He fanned us, never himself, keeping the air stirring. We would have had our baths, dressed in fresh clothes, and there would be the faint scent of violets about Lurie; Anson smelled of hand soap, and I emitted an odor of whatever fragrance Lurie saw fit to touch me with—Lilac Vegetal, and one day a week, Lucky Tiger. If I emitted fumes of Lucky Tiger, she had just given me a haircut. As this happened weekly, it was always a small clipping. Lurie eschewed face powders, out of deference to Anson's saying, "When I bite somebody, I want to taste raw meat." He had three classifications for osculation: a kiss, a bite, and a smack.

From Anson I received a couple of bites on the neck a day. Several smacks landed almost anywhere: cheek, forehead, nose. One night, in the swing, he informed me he'd been keeping count and that I owed him 283 smacks, and didn't I want to pay back 3 of them right now? That evening we had donned our sleeping garments. I was in my nightshirt, Lurie was in her lacy nightgown down to her ankles, and Anson in his pajamas. His pajama jacket was unbuttoned, so I reached over and touched my lips to his chest three times.

He said nothing for a moment, then said, "There are other places."

On many such evenings, some of them moonlit, we sat thus, Anson telling us of events of the day, of the latest on the Knuckleheads, of the tales of Pop Cod, of the three Little Jacks, of how both Chinaberry and the Bent Y Ranch came about. Presently I would get sleepy. Anson would lift me into his lap and draw

Lurie closer. Once he ascertained I was asleep, he would place me in Lurie's lap, and depending on how her hair was groomed for the day, unloose the plait or withdraw the hairpins and combs, put them in his shirt or pajama pockets, or hang them on the loops of the porch-swing chains. I had not always succumbed to slumber when this last happened.

For those hot nights, we slept on fresh sheets and pillowcases, our heads on pillows sweetened by the sun. The nightshirts first made for me had been replaced by pajamas modeled on Anson's. Not long after, they noticed that for several nights I had waked dripping with perspiration, pajamas sweated through. Despite her training as a nurse, it did not occur to Lurie to check my temperature. Then she remembered that my regular naps were lasting the afternoon through. I lay abed in the morning even after my face and hands had been washed. So something was wrong with me.

Lurie finally put a thermometer in my mouth on a Saturday morning. It read 102 degrees. After cooling the instrument and trying again, she got the same reading. The thermometer was then inserted anally. I was 102 at both ends. Anson was alarmed.

The grippe was unlikely in hot weather, but there were typhoid and dengue fever to consider, not to mention Rocky Mountain spotted fever. During all their searches, they'd never discovered a tick on me. Dengue was common in low-lying East Texas, in swampy areas of the coast, and had occurred when visitors brought it with them from Mississippi and Louisiana. There hadn't been a typhoid case in Inman or Robertson counties for five years. Who could say what I might have picked up sleeping on lumber piles, in churchyards, and on damp ground while crossing from Alabama? Or brought with me from home?

Everything went by the boards. Anson called the doctor's office in Bluewater to be certain he was in and to announce we were on our way. He called the Towerhouse and ordered that Ernest be found wherever he might be and sent to meet us at the office. If it was not known where Ernest was at the moment, all available hands were to search for him. Lurie undressed me and placed me in the tub for a quick bath. Hurriedly clothed, Anson grabbed me up, without socks or shoes, and fairly ran to the Overland car. My feet would not touch the ground that whole day. I was placed in Lurie's lap, and the car sprang out of the yard. Before we reached the mailbox, Lurie realized that Anson was in no condition to drive. She had him pull off, and they exchanged places. Anson buried his face against my neck and kept murmuring, "You'll be all right. You'll be all right."

They had not far to seek Ernest. He had been in the horse barn grooming a mare. He, Anson's mother, and Bronson were sitting in the waiting room when we arrived. For Ernest to witness my being carried was embarrassment enough, and when the doctor summoned Anson into his office for prior consultation, he plunked me into Ernest's lap. I would have been willing to die on the spot rather than this.

"Feeling bad, Skybo?" Ernest asked, feigning not to be worried. I shut my eyes, trying to imagine myself elsewhere. I could not. How Cadillac and Rance would laugh at this scene. As if he read my mind, Ernest said, "We won't let the Knuckleheads in on this, will we?"

I nodded with gratitude.

The doctor would see me alone. Anson left the examining room with protests, but he left.

The doctor knew of me already. Anything that happened at Chinaberry, or to do with the Winters family, became common knowledge. My temperature had retreated to 100 degrees.

"Sore here?" he asked, pressing my stomach.

No.

My knee jerk was normal.

"Do you want to go home?" he asked.

I didn't reply. Instead, tears flooded my eyes. The doctor handed me a paper handkerchief to dry them before he opened the door to admit Anson. I was to return the next day with a sample of feces.

I was brought back the following day. The feces were examined, and a diagnosis was made. "Worm fever," the doctor said. "Suffering from *Oxyuris vermicularis*. That means pinworms."

What followed was that Rosetta's and Angelica's families had to provide feces samples, too, as well as Lurie and Anson. So did Ernest and the Knuckleheads. The entire Chinaberry community. I was the only victim.

"Alabama worms, then," the doctor pronounced. "He brought them with him."

On the ride home the next day, Anson hummed a little joyous song that I did not recognize.

During my sickness, I regressed. Hardheaded as I was, with a mind of my own, I was unused to being made much of, and I came to enjoy it. I was unused to caresses, lifting, being carried about. I let Anson spoon-feed me when he believed I should eat a bit more, after all. I allowed them to dress and undress me. They constantly checked my forehead to see if I was cold or hot. Even after I got better, I still regressed.

I got to the point that I expected to go to sleep nightly in his lap, in a rocking chair, or sitting on the side of the bed, or in the porch swing. On a few oppressively hot nights when they slept on a mattress on the screened porch, I lay beside Anson. For a few minutes he would switch me over him to the middle, and when I turned toward Lurie, who smelled of violets, I laid my head on her breast. More than once he said, "I'm getting jealous," and returned me to the other side.

When we were in their room, I sometimes had to get up to relieve myself. I stumbled over their brass bed, and he'd awake to make sure I was all right. When I returned, I'd put my hand on his pillow to let him know I was back, and he'd tuck me in beside him and say, "Is the baby lonesome?" On waking, I'd be back in my own bed.

CHAPTER

Buffalo Wallow

"THIS BOY'S PAPA is giving me the devil about bringing him home to go to school," Ernest told Anson.

There was never any question about my attending; the problem was where. Some six miles to the east was a county-supported secondary school at a hamlet called Veasey, with some eighty enrolled, all the children of cotton growers. A third of these boarded in town during the week, as the distance was too great for walking and the farmers had no spare horses for transportation. Lurie or Blunt could drive me to and fro.

The Veasey School was not to Anson's liking. The teachers were daughters of the area who'd had a bit of training at one of the colleges and were mostly old maiden aunts. Deprived by their rural upbringing, they imposed their deprivation upon the students, and Anson would not have that for me.

There was another choice—Buffalo Wallow. The Wallow School was just across the Robertson County line, fully nine miles on the road to the Bent Y Ranch, and two miles farther on a side road, long abandoned by the county in upkeep and abandoned of support by the Board of Education when the number of students lowered to eight. They were now up to eleven. Ernest wrote to my father that I was attending the best school in the State of Texas and that Alabama could not boast its like.

Surprisingly enough, Ernest may have been right. The ranchers in the area were all of some means, so they hired their own teacher, a man, and one who met every expectation. He was a young married professor with two crawling children and was very devoted to his calling. They kept his salary a whet above any other, kept a cow fresh in milk in his lot, a beef to slaughter, a pig in his pen, and any surpluses from their fields and gardens were dumped at his gate. Save for the isolation, lack of telephone, and a road fairly impassable after a rain, what other was there to wish for? The young professor was even given a car—a Reo—which was nearing the end of its mechanical life and sounded like a threshing machine.

The Buffalo Wallow School was distant and inconvenient, yet it had the advantage of Anson's delivering me on his way to the ranch and picking me up in the afternoon. This, however, could last only until the fall roundup, when the daylight shortened and Anson's working hours almost doubled. Blunt and Lurie would have to take up the chore when that occurred.

The schoolhouse, newly painted and reshingled, stood in a slight depression that had been a wallowing ground from ancient times for buffalo. Otherwise, the land stretched as far as the eye could see, flat as a carpenter's level. The professor's domicile sat nearby. There was nothing between it and the horizon. The world seemed three-quarters sky. The professor's little home and the schoolhouse and the live oaks that sheltered it from the sun were all there was.

As the single new student, I brought the enrollment up to a dozen, and I was the only one to arrive by car. The other eleven came on horseback. Often a couple at a time came on horseback, and sometimes a pony supported three on its back. This school was like no other in the county, I was told. The seats were new, without a scratch or a carving. There were freestanding charts and maps, and the blackboards were at three levels. The walls were decorated with framed pictures of George Washington and the Alamo, along with the students' drawings and papers that had received good marks. When I asked Anson what this subscription school cost for a student, he said, "Not enough—worth more than it's costing." And then, "The teacher is the main thing."

Both Anson and Lurie took me that first day. When Professor Lewis asked my name to enroll me, Anson spoke up and said, "Anson."

"Anson, Junior?" the professor asked.

"You can list him so," Anson answered.

So I had lost my name. Besides, nobody except Ernest had spoken it since I'd left Alabama. The Knuckleheads had created a variety of nicknames on the way out, the most frequent being "Short Stuff" and "Little Doc."

The professor had no need to ask, as news of my presence had penetrated to the farthest ends of the county. Even the children knew of me, and they smiled at first when my odd Alabama brogue reached their ears. Although all of their grandfathers had brought their ways of speaking from different areas of the country, their speech had now melded to the uniform pattern for Robertson County, Texas.

What grade had I completed at school, I was asked. The fifth, was my reply. Judging by my size, the teacher doubted it, but he would give me a try. And so he was to do. I was above my grade in reading skills, below it in arithmetic. This last would be remedied, both by his ministrations and by Anson's.

When I was to sign my name on a lesson, I hesitated. My pencil was poised, but the professor must have read the turmoil in my head and said, "Just write it." I did. I signed it "Anson, Jr."

When this paper was shown to Anson by Lurie, he smiled, and great tears gathered in his eyes. He picked me up and walked up and down the hall several times.

In the Buffalo Wallow School that year, three students were beginners, one was in the eighth grade, the others scattered between. I was alone in the sixth. The professor sat beside me or stood beside me at the blackboard to hear my recitation or correct my figuring. For an hour a day, he taught us all together in history and geography, his instructions fitting both the young and the older. When I recited, the others were all eyes and ears. I remained a curiosity.

For one thing, Anson's instructions to the professor were that I should have a half-hour nap at one in the afternoon. A carriage blanket and a cushion were supplied for it, and I slept on the floor of the cloakroom. The recess period was moved to fit this schedule. Another thing was Anson's sometimes reappearance a half hour after he had delivered me; he had come back to take me with him for the day.

I have no idea of the reason he gave the professor. To me he'd say, "I want you with me."

Those days we went elsewhere than the ranch. To town, where he had business in the courthouse. Or to the hardware store. Or to rest awhile at the livery stable.

"Lurie would be bothered if we told her," he said, which was my cue to not tell her.

Still, Lurie learned of it and said nothing. What was good for Anson was good for her. Lurie's sister had heard of it on the telephone from some of the other parents, who had heard of my occasional disappearances from my classmates.

Getting me to school on time meant waking me early, and as the days shortened and the business at the ranch quickened, I began to be driven to school by Blunt, sometimes by Lurie.

When Lurie took me, she stopped just short of the schoolyard and kissed me good-bye, and she let me hold my arms around her neck longer, without pulling away, than she did at home. She understood my ardent behavior for what it was—both abandonment and attraction.

A day came when Anson was slated to pick me up on the way home. He left word with Ellafronia at the Towerhouse to telephone Lurie at Chinaberry and have Blunt go for me after school instead. The lines were down over part of the route, and the Bluewater exchange agreed to forward the message through a second exchange, bypassing the affected area. The message didn't arrive, and Lurie was surprised at dusk when Anson drove up without me. Without getting out of the Hudson, Anson turned and raced back toward Buffalo Wallow.

When school had turned out at three-thirty, the professor took me home with him. His wife began preparing supper as soon as he turned up to watch after the two babies. The crawlers, if not twins, were within a year of each other, and they scooted over the floor like crawfish in a pond. As the afternoon faded and nobody came for me, I refused all entreaties to eat supper. A glass of milk and cookies were set before me anyhow, yet I declined. With dusk settling over the plains, I went into the yard and hung on the gate. Dark was fully accomplished when the headlights of the Hudson appeared, like two great eyes approaching. I did not run to meet Anson when he drew up. I let him come to me, to pull me loose from the gate. He saw instantly that I was swollen up with injury.

"Sorry, son," he said. "There was a mix-up."

I did not relent.

Anson did not pick me up. Holding my arm, he propelled me toward the house, where the Lewis family awaited. Walking into the lamp-lit room, he made his apologies for his tardiness, and noticing the two babies, he held his arms out to them. One came to him readily, but the other refused. I had never seen him touch a child, even Jack's youngest. Lurie had told me that in the days of his early grief, more than one child had been offered to him to fondle, and his reply had always been, "It doesn't belong to me."

Anson poked the baby's dimples and plucked his chin. Something rose inside me, from my stomach to my chest, my neglect forgotten. I was jealous.

"You've got two babies here," Anson said. "You don't need both, so I'll take this one."

The Lewises smiled at the joke.

Standing behind Anson I threw my arms around his legs impulsively. The tears came.

Anson restored the baby to the parents, picked me up, and started toward the car.

"Things get out of control once in a while," Anson told me, as we made our way to the car beneath the starry blue sky of evening. "Nobody's fault. My life has a record of them."

Blunt Arrow

"ALL OF THE OLD HEADS in this territory came from some-where else," Anson told me. "Papa came from Tennessee, and he remembers a little about living earlier than that as a child in North Carolina. Mostly he says he recalls his mother dressing him in shirttails. He remembers the plow horse named Bess and his father scratching out 'Oh! Susanna' on his fiddle."

Anson's brother Jack was such a great admirer of his father that, except for the interposition of his wife, all his children would have been named Jack in some combination. In the event, his second son was, and his three boys were nicknamed Little Jack, Jacky Boy, and Baby Jack.

In the wide neighborhood, this was something of a joke, and the considerable landholdings of the Winters family were re-ferred to as Jack Country. I was not wholly to escape.

While Grandma was the first to call me Little Anson, Anson himself, perhaps to please his father, perhaps as a nod to tradi-tion, referred to me sometimes as "My Jack." While this may be confusing to an outsider, everyone inside the family knew with-out explanation who was being talked about.

What I was to learn about this country came to me in bits and pieces, from various sources, beginning from my earliest mem-ories. Not only had my father spent three years farming near Killeen, Texas, but two of my uncles had followed, on hearing about the rich earth where cotton virtually jumped out of the ground. And my Aunt Ada, just turned sixteen, had eloped with a widower and headed west, never to return, even for a visit, until the year of Grandpa's death, 1925. And as a coincidence, her sister—who was actually named Texas—followed.

The Cyclopedia of Universal Knowledge had not a word to say about the blacklands of the state known as the Cotton Belt. How would it, as it was published in 1851 and was probably a quarter of a century in the making? A child could not know this: That buffalo and Indians possessed the black strip of earth, beginning just below Oklahoma Territory and running south for some four hundred miles past San Antonio, at its greatest width seventy-five miles, at its most narrow, twenty. In the whole of America, there was no other such fertile landmass, save smaller strips in Alabama and Mississippi. Black dirt, sticky as glue when wet, cracking like a broken windowpane when dry. Expandable clay.

Chambers County, in eastern Alabama, was north of this geological strip. There the land yielded, when supplemented with guano, at best a bale to the acre, at average, half a bale. Thus, the hearsay that Texas yielded two bales to the acre was a magnet to a generation of farmers, beginning in the years following the Civil War and extending well into the twentieth century.

At the time my source of wisdom, *The Cyclopedia of Universal Knowledge*, was being formulated, and prior to it, the blacklands were hunting grounds of the various tribes of Indians: the Arikara, the Pawnee, the Comanche, the Caddo. Historians have stated that the Caddo tribe—unlike the others roaming the plains—were a settled people, living in villages, cultivating their corn and beans and pumpkins.

In telling me his family's history, Anson stuck mostly to episodes of tension, the year when men died of typhoid, untended by physicians on their isolated farms and ranches. The summer he and his brother suffered a bout of dengue fever. The drought year. Tornadoes. Robertson County was referred to in the newspapers as Cyclone Alley. Most homes had some form of outdoor cellar the people repaired to when they deemed it necessary. We had one in Alabama called the flower pit. House and porch plants were placed there in winter below the frost line. The mention of cyclones troubled me. I had experienced one a couple years before and was lucky to be alive. If a black cloud appeared on the horizon, I became fearful. I had created a prayer that I uttered to myself over and over when a peal of thunder disturbed the sky: "Lord, preserve me . . . preserve me . . . preserve me."

If Anson told me how his father came by a section of Robertson County land, I have forgotten. I have forgotten much of what he told me in evenings in the swing, on trips I took with him, or perhaps it is still recorded in the tissues of my brain, awaiting some code word to bring it forth. I seem to remember more than most, and I have always been a good listener. "All ears," my mother said. When I was born, my mother thought my ears stuck out a bit farther than necessary. I had to wear a band about my head until my ears assumed an acceptable position.

A man by the name of Johnnes Tower had—one way or another, some thought legal—come by a sizable tract of land in Robertson County only eleven miles from Chinaberry. He was in the process of trying to acquire more to start up a ranch. Robertson County was where the geological miracle of black dirt ended, visibly, if you went by the green growing a half mile beyond Towerhouse, where fields of corn and millet and gardens flourished. Within a space of three hundred yards, scrubland began, the ground capable of supporting only cattle, and only then if they were kept on the move.

Another oddity, if not a miracle, was that Anson—Johnnes Anson Winters—was named for this man, not for Big Jack.

Grandma undoubtedly had a hand in the naming, to honor the man to whom they owed so much. Anson was her maiden name. She claimed Anson, the first governor of the Republic of Texas, as a forebear, though the line of kinship was not readily traceable. A day came when Johnnes Tower found it necessary to leave the country suddenly, overnight. A common thing in those unsettled days. He was a loner. No family, no relatives anybody knew about, no indication of where he had come from originally. But where there is money, even if secretly held, the news of it will get out. There being no established bank around, Johnnes Tower knew Big Jack had the gold certificates gained from the sale of the farm in West Tennessee hidden behind a loose plank in the floor. At that time, Big Jack had not married Maryellen Anson; he was batching with Bronson, his seventeen-year-old foster son, and raising cotton at Chinaberry.

It was a cliché situation—a man had killed another, or wronged someone grievously, and felt it wise to leave the area until anger cooled or time healed. There is probably not a county or a town in the State of Texas where this had not occurred, in some, more than once. Disappearances, while infrequent, were not a wonder. A recent migrant would often be stricken with yearning for Georgia, the hills of Kentucky, or the meadows of Dan in Virginia, and would strike out without a word.

Johnnes Tower arrived at Chinaberry past midnight on horseback, and he had with him a court clerk bearing the seal of Texas, empowered to make deeds. When it became evident Big Jack did not have money enough to purchase the whole of Tower's land, a deal was struck, to wit: Big Jack would be deeded half, the land on the east; the western half would be his effective ten years hence if Tower did not return to claim it.

Tower imposed a condition. He had a squatter, a Comanche. He was the only Indian known to be living in the blacklands.

Most people had never seen one, the last of them being driven out or resettled in Oklahoma long ago. This Comanche was called Wounded Deer, and he had with him a grandson some twenty years of age. The aged Comanche had no command of English, but his grandson, who called himself Little Wounded Bear and came to be known as Blunt, had in some way learned the language. The old Indian had said, "I have come here to die. My father died here, and I will follow him." And then, mysteriously: "I am my father."

In later years, Blunt had told Big Jack about the song his grandfather sang:

> I am my father's sons.
> I am my father recreated.
> Therefore I am he.
> I will die where he died.

Tower's request was that this aged Indian be allowed to accomplish his days on the ranch and that Big Jack take the young buck into his employ. Tower rode off into the night, followed by the clerk, and was never seen or heard of again. During the ten years when Big Jack's hold on the ranch was tenuous at best, considering he had paid out his last dollar, Big Jack lived part-time at Chinaberry and part-time at the ranch, gradually buying stock and starting a herd, working hand in hand with Bronson. They could hardly say themselves how they had managed. They hired help as needed or when they could afford it. Big Jack eventually married Maryellen and fathered a daughter and two sons. After ten years had passed, he renamed the ranch, calling it the Bent Y, even though the house was still referred to as Towerhouse.

Blunt had indicated one day that he would take a journey to his people and would be gone from the dark of the moon to the full. When he returned, he brought a wife and two children with him. They spoke both English and Spanish. One child was José, who now had children of his own—a godsend to a family in need of cotton pickers. The mother had given her surname as Martinez. To register to vote, Little Wounded Bear became Blunt Martinez—borrowing his wife's surname.

Blunt was already an old man when Anson and Jack were children. Or so it appeared. From year to year, he seemed not to grow any older. This man, with skin like the leather he worked into harnesses, saddle, and shoes, seemed ageless, impervious to change. He could tell you he was born in Arizona the year of the long winter, the year the Great Spirit hid the buffalo and members of the tribe died of starvation, including his mother and brother. His father had walked out into a blizzard in search of food and never returned. A few members of the tribe had survived by boiling buffalo robes for nutrients. When that was, he could not say. Little Wounded Bear, Blunt, must have been nearing Big Jack's age. How his great-grandfather happened to die in what was now Robertson County, he had no knowledge.

Blunt and his Mexican wife had children, and the children in their late teens went away. Two sons left, to where could not be ascertained, for, as Anson said, "Never ask an Indian, even a part one, why, when, or wherefore." They later returned with Spanish-speaking wives—Angelica and Rosetta—and began to work for Anson.

As the cattle herd increased in size at the Bent Y, Blunt became more and more in charge of the cotton crops at Chinaberry. Yet by the time Anson and Jack were out of rompers, José had taken over this duty, and the aging Blunt became watchdog at Chinaberry house.

This had come about in part because of the anxiety of Big Jack for children. His own younger brother, playing alone, had somehow gotten tangled in a harness and died of asphyxiation. Had an adult been by, rescuing would have been simple. And as he and Bronson were so often away, there needed to be some reliable man on the place just in case of anything untoward happening.

"Keep your eye on these boys," Big Jack had told Blunt, and Blunt took the order to heart. From the time they were old enough to step outside the house, there was Blunt. Wherever they might ramble, to the barns, to the fields, Blunt followed at a distance, as if he just happened to be going in that direction. On many occasions, they had tried to hide from him, but Anson said you couldn't hide from an Indian. They came in time to buddy with him. They went horseback to school, and he was there waiting on his mount for them to emerge when school took out. Once, when they had shimmied up the steep roof of the cotton house to its peak before he could reach them, he had called them down, catching them as they slid across the metal roof. "If anything happened to you, I'd have to kill myself," he said, a warning I was to hear myself. As long as he had known him, Anson said, he had never had a conversation with him. His black eyes darted about. He anticipated you, knew what you wanted before you said it. "Many's the time I've decided I'll take a trot on Blue as soon as I reach home, before supper," Anson said. "I'll drive in and there's Blue, curried and combed and saddled up."

One evening, as the three of us sat in the swing with me in the middle, Lurie asked Anson to tell me about the passing of Blunt's grandfather, Wounded Deer. Anson had to say that the story had got rusty in his mind since he last heard it himself.

"I'll have to ask Papa," he said. "Papa never forgot anything he ever heard." Old Jack had heard it from Blunt's wife, and how she had got so many words out would remain a mystery. Blunt's wife had died before Anson and Jack were born. Where he had buried her was not to be known.

It was my turn now to be guarded and followed by Blunt. He was behind me when I met the mail hack at the end of the lane on Saturday, in hopes of a letter from home. When I played roly-hole marbles in the yard, he sat on the lumber pile and mended harnesses, sewed moccasins, or did scrollwork on leather with an awl. During those lonesome days when Lurie was busy at her sewing machine or with her embroidery or tatting, there was Blunt nearby, and he was a comfort.

CHAPTER Twelve

Bluebonnets

FROM THE TENDER beginning of a few "smacks," there was an increase to many. Mine were smacks; Lurie's were kisses. By Anson's definition, a smack was a light touching of the lips to a forehead, a chin, a cheek. Besides lifting me to greet me, he often pitched me into the air and caught me. As a prank, he sometimes carried me upside down and talked to my feet. The occasional red spots that turned up on my neck were whisker burns. Lurie chided him and treated my neck with cloverine salve.

Three times a week Lurie shaved Anson with a straight razor, and using the brush, he would lather my jaws, take out his pocketknife, and scrape it off.

"Practicing up for the future," he would say. He brought home a new contraption, a Gillette razor, and began shaving himself the days between. That ended the razor burns.

For me, as for Anson and Lurie, there were freshly laundered garments every day. The gasoline-powered washing machine operated almost daily. We slept on fresh sheets and pillowcases all the months of August and September.

During the weeks of August, when Anson could come home before dark, or on a rare day in mid-afternoon, we would sit in the porch swing awaiting his arrival. Lurie would have begun her toilet an hour earlier. I remember her freshly ironed dress, usually one of her own making, her cheeks lightly rouged and powdered, the scent of violets about her. Her golden hair, so frequently shampooed and brushed to a gleam by Angelica, would be done up in one of the various modes taught in a beauty course—hanging to the shoulder and caught up by a ribbon, or in large woven plaits or a bun on her head, secured by hairpins and combs.

Lest one might think Lurie too good to work, as the gossip had it about Anson's first wife, this was hardly the case. Lurie sewed and crocheted and tatted. Every bureau wore a sample of her handicraft. One task she did herself, save when heavy lifting was involved, was the making of beds. She made up their bed and my own every day. Mattresses and goose-feather pillows were often taken out to sun. I was to learn that the fragrance enhancing Lurie and Anson's brass bed was from sachets tucked inside the pillowcases. On occasion Lurie dusted and swept, but not regularly, as this was left for Rosetta. Nor did she ever enter the parlor, where the blinds were drawn and the door kept locked. This was Anson's place. Though latched, a skeleton key was in the lock, ready for turning.

I know it was locked, because I turned the knob once and did not dare do more. I was curious, my curiosity soon turning to a mild obsession.

Once, when the washing machine was short of fuel, Lurie was at a tub helping with the wash when Blunt thought to siphon gasoline from a truck. He couldn't stand to see her working that hard. We all worshipped her.

Lurie was not, admittedly, a country wife with hair strung about her face, rushing to the cookstove and the scrub brush, awaiting a husband coming in from ranch or field, a husband wearing pants with dirt enough in them to stand alone, the underarms of his shirt whitened by salt from evaporated sweat.

Lurie was not this kind of woman. Nor was I the boy just in from a torrid day in an Alabama cotton field.

In the evenings, waiting in the swing, I was as primped as a boy can be, thanks to Lurie. I was shining, bathed, my face and neck scrubbed raw. My fingernails had been scratched under and filed. I wore a shirt and wash pants of Lurie's making. My hair was slicked down, parted on the right side as Anson thought it ought to be. I was, in Alabama parlance, "stinking clean." My sisters would have called me a mess.

Sitting in the swing, ears alert to the first sounds of Anson's approaching car, which could be heard from a mile away, Lurie told me many stories, mostly about Anson. She believed that to understand him was to appreciate him. It was obvious for a long time that I had not yet overcome my diffidence and fully accepted his affection. But she continued to describe her first attraction to Anson at age twelve, the empty years when she could barely sustain her hope, and their subsequent marriage.

It must have relieved some lingering anxiety on Lurie's part to talk about him, to have him understood. With whom else could she talk? Not with Angelica or Rosetta, who lived in a different world. Not with Anson's people, with whom circumspection was the rule and self-revelation unthinkable. She would have me know that Anson was a "good man." She would often look off across the fields and repeat, quietly, "He has a pure heart."

One evening, as we sat there dressed up and awaiting Anson's arrival, she told me about Anson's first visit to the child's grave, to engage my sympathy and understanding. The particulars of her story could have been known only by an outsider, as no member of the Winters family would have revealed these particulars, so I must assume that her account of the day's events came from Ellafronia, who had been privy to all of the Winters family secrets since she arrived to serve at Towerhouse.

Following the death of Little Johnnes, Anson stayed for months at the ranch, under the eye of his mother, under everybody's eye. While he was not by nature self-destructive, they feared for him. Had not a cowboy on one of the ranches nearby, on the death of his young wife, put a shotgun his mouth and pulled the trigger? At the start, Anson stayed nights at Jack's house nearby, where it was thought the three Little Jacks would be some distraction. They were only a reminder, and after a single night, he fled to the big house. Anson's brother Jack, thinking to cheer him, had picked up the youngest of the three Little Jacks and placed him in Anson's arms. Anson had set the child aside, saying, "He's not my baby."

As Blunt had watched over Anson and Jack as children, now it was the turn of Pop Cod, the aging cowpoke, to take up that duty. Anson often stepped out the door, wandering about the several barns, the feeder calf pens, the lots where brood mares with their foals were enclosed, and he would watch the antics of the young bull—and during all this, Pop Cod was watching. When Anson sometimes saddled up and rode for an hour on the ranch land, Pop Cod, for all the difficulty in mounting at his age, followed behind.

Pop Cod had been in on the establishment of the Bent Y. The first cowboy hired, in fact. He was Big Jack's age. He had gotten too old for the job, as had his boss. The ranch had expanded in size from a half-hundred cattle to a herd requiring six cowboys, three at a time, spelling each other on a regular schedule. Pop Cod had no admitted relatives. When asked, he had replied, "Orphaned. Kicked out the back door." Pop Cod lived in the bunkhouse, a couple hundred yards behind Towerhouse. He kept the bunkhouse in a semblance of order, and he had charge of the tack room.

"What he doesn't know about harnesses and saddles hasn't been discovered yet," I was told.

But foremost, Pop Cod kept Big Jack out of mischief. They spent at least an hour most days on the porch of the bunkhouse, whittling and reminiscing about the days when the West was truly wild and woolly, legend and fact.

In his grief, Anson sat at a table at Towerhouse and did not eat. He lost weight. His mother poked food into his mouth as one might a child's, as he later served me when he thought I hadn't eaten enough. He lay abed nights and did not sleep. A light was kept burning, and when he arose in the night and walked about, someone else arose and was attentive. The household took turns. Ofttimes it was Ellafronia's turn.

And the story she had told about Anson visiting Little Johnnes's grave zigged and zagged as Lurie retold it to me, going further into the past. I ate up every bit of it.

Upon our arrival at Chinaberry, I had noticed that there was no dog that came out to greet us, as there would have been at any home back in Alabama. Lurie said there was a reason for this.

When he was six, Anson had come by a puppy. He had fed it, watered it, informed all and sundry it was his property, and sneaked it into bed with him at night. The pup went to school with him, awaited him at the door. Anson carried two lunches to school, one for himself, one for the dog. Then this beloved animal disappeared, and young Anson was inconsolable. The search was wide, advertised in the county paper, and a sizable reward was offered. Anson grieved for the longest while.

At a later time, it was surmised that the animal had fallen into a well dug in a nearby pasture, now served by a windmill.

The water came out briny, and the well was covered over for a time until it could be filled in. The dog had probably wormed its way under the metal cover and become trapped. Lurie reported Anson's mother as saying, "When Anson loves something or somebody, he holds on too tight. He won't let loose."

For nearly a month, Anson never mentioned Little Johnnes to anyone. But both in his fitful sleep and even sitting up, wide awake in bed, he would call to him: "Baby, baby, oh my baby." Nor did he suggest going to the cemetery. He must have known he was not ready. Then one day, he mentioned Beech Ledge to his mother.

"Someday," she had replied. "Not now."

Anson insisted, yet not too strenuously. So they reached an agreement. He could go within three months. She had him make the promise. When the three months were up, she put him off another month, until the first of May. They were all watching over him as tenderly as they could, after all. Even Big Jack had softened. He would sometimes put a hand on Anson's shoulder and say, "My son, my son," just the way Anson mourned for his own son in his sleep and in his waking dreams. They kept all the guns locked up, standing by helplessly as Anson lost more and more weight.

But time heals to some degree. Anson began to improve, and he even gained back the pounds he lost. Everybody in the household started to sleep without expectation of alarm. Pop Cod gave up his vigil. Anson eventually rode out to the herd and did not return for a week. A cowboy returning from his stint reported Anson was his old self again. He had taken a turn at night watch; he had actually laughed at some of the jokes cracked around the campfire. He was only restrained, and he did not join in when they sang, with mouth-harp accompaniment, "Tenting Tonight on the Old Camp Ground." A sad song.

Yet the Winters household was tense on the day Anson was to go to Beech Ledge. Anson had slept in his clothes the night before, sat up staring outside into the early spring drizzle. By six o'clock he had bathed and shaved and had donned his Sunday cowboy attire. The weather cleared as if for him. His boots shone. The solid silver buckle of his wide belt—fashioned by Blunt and worn only on special occasions—possessed the sign of the Bent Y Ranch, and it shone with the boots when it caught sunlight. His wearing of the belt buckle was somehow troubling to his mother, so she kept an eye on the gun rack that morning, fearing he might take a pistol with him to lie down beside Little Johnnes's grave and do something she would not be able to bear.

They had planned to go together: Anson, his mother, Big Jack, Jack, and Bronson. There was a bouquet of bluebonnets to be taken. But, no, Anson wanted to go alone. After some palaver, he allowed Bronson to accompany him. They set off in a truck, as the night's rain had muddied the roads. There is no mud so successful as Texas mud. The earth was so soft that the truck created deeper ruts as it went. Anticipating this day, Jack had taken a couple of hands to clean up the cemetery a week earlier. The child's grave was still covered with mounded dirt, and a marble slab to match his mother's was sitting three feet away, awaiting the settling of the earth about the casket.

A short piece before they reached the cemetery, Anson asked Bronson to stop. The road had lost all semblance of being a road and was more like a trail. He said he would go on alone. Of the members of the family, Bronson had more confidence than the others that Anson only needed time. He would adjust, Bronson said. Bronson was old enough that he treated Jack and Anson as his sons, and you will remember they unaccountably resembled him. Bronson leaned against the car and watched as Anson disappeared behind the towering live oaks that hid the cemetery.

Bronson, from long practice as a cowboy, retrieved his field glasses from the truck when Anson did not return within a half hour. Walking to the right, to get a view of the graves, he saw Anson kneeling, one hand on Melba's marble slab, the other upon Little Johnnes's mound. The bluebonnets rested on the child's grave. Bronson returned to the truck and put the field glasses back into the glove compartment. No reason to hurry Anson, he thought. Let him have it out with a grief nobody could truly share.

Anson's mother, from the moment Anson and Bronson had driven off, had become restive. As time passed, she grew more disturbed and paced the floor, wringing her hands. Within less than twenty minutes, she and Jack had called Ellafronia to join them, and all had piled into a car, driving to the cemetery. There was nothing else to do.

On reaching Bronson, who was parked near the cemetery, they all jumped out, and Bronson waved them back. "He's all right," he yelled, softly. "I've checked."

They waited another thirty minutes before they all approached the cemetery, quietly and on foot.

Anson lay stretched upon Little Johnnes's mound, his arms half-buried in the mud, reaching down. He was asleep. Blossoms of the bluebonnets were stuck to his face like stars.

CHAPTER Thirteen

The Bull Run

THE WINTERS FAMILY was an open-hearted group of people, even if they did not seem so to the casual onlooker. They owned gifts of the earth—land, cattle—and had money in the bank. They were not grasping, not asking for more. They had come by it hard, yet it had not hardened them.

Many thought the Winterses were strange, not easy to know. The womenfolk did not "hang on the telephone," which meant they had no confidantes. Any news of them was difficult to come by. On the paternal side, they were a transplanted Appalachian family. Big Jack's speech bore the imprint of his early years in Western North Carolina, with a dash of West Tennessee. As for the maternal side—who knew? Anson's mother had said that Big Jack had "carried her off" when she was not much more than a child of sixteen and he almost twice her age. "I didn't even love him," she'd say, "then." But she came to love him, and she came to love the Bent Y Ranch, where they eventually set up house-keeping after leaving Chinaberry.

The Bent Y had begun from scratch, ranch land without so much as a cow. A few mavericks were branded, and among the calves there came a bull of stamina and quality. This bull set the standard for the short-legged, stocky longhorns that became the trademark of the Bent Y. But fashions in cattle change, bulls have their day, and ranch owners have eyes out for a male to up-grade their stock. They want less fat, more lean, all endurance.

In the first year Big Jack added the ranch to his undertakings, and for a dozen succeeding years, the profits from Chinaberry's cotton crop were invested in livestock. As the cattle began to turn a profit, the earnings for both were used to buy more land and extend the borders of the ranch.

From the beginning, Big Jack, Bronson (who was in his twen-ties at the time the ranch was started), and Blunt tended the growing herd. They were soon to be joined by Pop Cod. Within a half-dozen years, the ranch reached its limits in the north and south. No more land was for sale or apt to be.

To the west was free range, where many herds grazed and to where the Bent Y drifted its herd at the end of summer when the grass there was most abundant, and as Big Jack put it, the cattle could be "brought into case" for fall shipment. On free range, any stray animal happened upon was promptly branded. It was a common practice, justified by the knowledge that other herds-men were branding strays from other herds. In this way there was fair trade.

One day Anson told me he had word that three antelopes had joined the herd, and when the cattle were close enough to reach and return in a day, he would take me there on horseback. By then there were two herds on the ranch, the smaller of which had the antelopes and was grazing just inside Bent Y property. The other was far afield, on free range that the Bent Y punchers referred to as "Japan."

The second time I was taken to the Towerhouse, I asked Pop Cod if the antelopes were branded as were the regular stock. It had always been said of me back home that I asked too many questions, and irritating ones, as they were usually ones to which nobody knew the answer. But Pop Cod knew.

"No," he said, sitting propped in his chair on the bunkhouse porch. "I always liked to see them grazing. If you have to look at a bunch of brutes all day, it's good to rest your eyes on something different. Like looking at women instead of men."

What Pop Cod didn't tell me, but Anson did later, was that a request came in once from Austin, asking for two antelopes, one of each sex. That had been back during Pop Cod's active days. With some difficulty, they were lassoed and delivered, to be placed in a zoo or possibly a traveling circus. Pop Cod was to regret this to the end of his life, which was less than a month away from the day I asked him my question.

One of the topics of conversation often heard among cattlemen is the location of a prize bull, one with the qualities to be bred into a herd. "No bull, no ranch" was a saying.

When stockmen attend cattle shows, which either Jack or Anson or both did regularly, they have an eye out for such an animal, either to appreciate what God and man have wrought in the way of breeding or to bargain for them. Such was the trip the two brothers took to Waco in October.

Jack was to bring the cattle truck from the ranch to Chinaberry, which was roughly on the way, pick up Anson, and drive to Waco and back, all in a single day. This would require their leaving before daylight and returning in the early hours of Sunday morning.

This was Saturday, a day of no school and no mail, and I was glad of the first and sorrowful of the second. Jack arrived at Chinaberry when it was still dark, and I was wakened by the noise of the truck rack as it entered the yard. Jack carried in his arms his sleeping eldest son, Little Jack, and placed him fully clothed on the side of my bed.

As he pulled off Little Jack's shoes and loosened his clothing, he told us that Little Jack had determined to go to Waco with them and couldn't be talked out of it. Such a trip, and the purpose of it, was out of the question for a ten-year-old.

"He'll cry a little when he wakes up," Jack said, "but he'll get over it. He'll be all right. When he starts playing with Little Anson, he'll forget all about it."

I was sitting up in bed, wide-eyed. Anson had told me before I went to sleep that he would be gone when I waked and I would be slumbering again before he returned. It had never occurred to me that I might go along.

Anson lifted me up and asked, "You're not going to cry, are you?"

I shook my head no. I was only partially awake and was almost back to sleep when he put me down.

Little Jack waked me with his crying later that morning. Lurie appeared with a pan of warm water and a washcloth, and throwing open the blinds, she washed both our faces and hands as we sat up in bed.

When Little Jack kept crying, Lurie asked him what he wanted.

"My Dad-o," he replied.

Fifteen minutes later we were at the table, our chins hovering over bowls of cornflakes and milk, Little Jack grinning. To my eyes he was a young version of Bronson, his foster uncle, even more so than he was of Jack and Anson. The resemblance was too notable to overlook.

Two years younger, Little Jack was a third larger in size than I was. When Blunt lifted us up by the seat of our pants and hung us on the steelyards, Little Jack weighed eighty-one. I weighed seventy-three, a four-pound gain from when I had arrived at Chinaberry. The candy Anson was sneaking to me, the morsel he poked into my mouth with a fork after I had stopped eating, was showing up. The day Lurie found a stick of licorice in my pocket she claimed to know it all along. "The smell of licorice hangs on like garlic," she had said. The condition Anson had set for consuming the candy he slipped to me, even after the discovery, was waiting until after supper, not before. To begin with, it was a play-secret, known to the three of us.

This was Little Jack's first extended visit to Chinaberry. We explored the house, entering every room across the hall except the locked one with the key hanging in the door. We climbed to the rafters in the cotton house and jumped into the great mound as soft as snow. We climbed the ladder into the barn loft to see what was there. We sat in the wooden swing under the chinaberry trees, facing each other to give it balance and make it rise higher than was wise, until Blunt—who all the while was keeping an eye on us—came to scotch the swing with a hand. And every hour or so, when it came to mind again, Little Jack cried for his father. In his view, his father had tricked him, abandoned him in his sleep. I began to agree with him, to join him in his moody moment, to feel that Anson should have taken me as well. Little Jack wept; I only puffed up in injury.

With her own hands, despite Angelica and Rosetta's presence, Lurie fixed us a picnic dinner of cold chicken and homemade bread, sweet potato custard, and lemonade. We ate under a tent we raised under the shade cast by the crepe myrtles. After an hour's nap on pallets on the screened back porch, we played roly-hole marbles, and then Blunt had ready for us bows made of Osage orange limbs and cane arrows, so we played Indians Chasing Sheepherders. Sheepherders were considered the dirt of the earth in Robertson County. Occasionally, Little Jack paused long enough to cry, with me accompanying him in gloom if not in tears.

In late afternoon, Little Jack wanted to walk down the lane to the road, the way Jack and Anson would be coming. He was aware that the return would be far into the night. We might have gone farther had not Blunt whistled at us and motioned us back.

We were asleep again, in my trundle bed, after midnight, when the travelers returned. Again I awakened and learned the trip had been a dry run. No bull had been purchased, for the prices were out of line.

"Did the boy cry?" Jack asked Lurie.

Lurie had to admit that he did. "But only a little," she said. "They played all day, hardly had a dull moment."

Jack wrapped his sleeping son in a carriage blanket, declining all invitations to spend the rest of the night, declaring he had to be home at daybreak.

I was sitting up in bed, awake enough to remember that Anson had been remiss in not taking me with him. He picked me up. I swelled up like a toad, like only a neglected boy could.

Hurriedly Lurie complimented me. "Little Jack cried but our boy didn't," she said.

Anson studied me a moment. "Did you want to cry?" he asked.

I shook my head yes. It couldn't be denied.

"You can cry now," he said.

And I did.

CHAPTER

Irena

CHINABERRY WAS A PLACE bursting with stories, and there was another that I was told, which deserves to be told now—the story of Irena Kendrick, the sister of Anson's first wife, Melba.

Irena was a year and a day younger than Melba. From infancy their mother had dressed them alike. Dresses, hats, slippers, ribbons. So twinlike many could not tell them apart. You never saw one without the other. Anson became acquainted with them the last two years he attended Bluewater High School. Melba was a classmate, Irena a grade behind. At age sixteen, when all was innocence and fun, Anson "went with" both of them. There was no chance of seeing either alone, their father being as much a stickler in the matter as the mother.

Following graduation, Anson attended Texas A & M for two years, his courses vaguely connected to agricultural science. The Kendrick sisters, the year after Irena's completing high school, attended for a term a finishing school in Armory, Mississippi, from whence their parents had migrated. There they were expected to brush up on Southern manners and decorum, learn a smattering of French, perfect their piano studies—which never did go much further than "Kitten on the Keys"—and be able to cross a room balancing a book on their heads. Lurie, who told me all I ever knew of the Kendricks, said the book should have been put into their heads rather than on top of it.

As had other immigrants, the Kendricks brought with them their own Central Mississippi culture. Too far north to be called Cajuns, too far South to qualify as hillbillies, the Kendricks had not truly left Mississippi. They brought it with them. They had the gazebo, the wide Southern verandah, the hammocks on the lawn, the heavy damask curtains, the straw-matted floors in summer, and the Turkish rugs in winter.

The girls' voices were soft and alluring to prospective suitors, who found the protectiveness of the parents formidable. They went nowhere except together, and with the chaperoning of the mother or a trusted elder female.

The Kendricks had the only house in the town with hired girls—two of them—to cook, launder, and do anything that, as neighbors believed, might soil Melba's or Irena's hands. This was not totally true. Tolbert Kendrick grew up hard on a farm west of Tupelo. He saw to it that his daughters assisted the hired girls, learned to sew and embroider, and especially to cook. Tolbert, who had become wealthy so suddenly, could not overcome the possibility that his money might vanish as quickly. Even to that day, some twenty-five years having passed, he expected claims against his uncle's estate, which never happened, and he never gave away anything in his life, except a daughter, and he came to regret that. As adverse as he was to relinquishing Melba and Irena to anyone, he saw no other course. He found it hard to accept that his town-raised daughters would be shut away on a farm. He had a built-in distrust of cowboys, real or ex.

During the term Melba and Irena spent at finishing school in Mississippi, their individuality evolved. They never dressed alike again. They no longer looked like twins. And while Melba was pretty, Irena was turning out to be the beauty. But if you were not looking at them, you'd never have known which one was speaking.

Quitting his academic career after two years was a decision made for Anson by Big Jack, his mother said, and Anson probably assented too readily because of the Kendrick girls. Where other suitors found it difficult to approach them, much less to get a date with one, Anson found nothing in his way—except, as events were to bear, he was in love with the both of them. Lurie's brother-in-law had once remarked, "Now if Anson was a Turk and lived in the Ottoman Empire, he could marry both and have it over with," to which her sister, Velvet, had rejoined, "They could join the Mormons and go live in Salt Lake City." Lurie had reminded her that the custom of multiple wives had passed.

Which one? was the conundrum of the hour, the day, for several years. It seemed a dilemma without resolution, but Tolbert Kendrick was too hardheaded an individual not to solve it.

Telephones were by now growing out from Bluewater and sprouting across the empty landscape, crossing county lines, linking up isolated farms and ranches, shrinking the desolation. Which one? became a taunting question in the minds of many a housewife who never saw a Winters or a Kendrick, and perhaps never would. But now they could be talked about, even though a call to Austin or San Antonio or Amarillo would go through one try in five times.

Before the news could be fairly digested or fully believed that Irena was dating a clerk in her father's hardware store, the word was that Anson had married Melba and they had gone to live at Chinaberry. It was firmly believed, and probably true, that Tolbert Kendrick had asked his younger daughter to step aside in favor of her elder sister. A few dates with the clerk, and then no more. Nobody expected her to "marry down" socially. Further proof that Tolbert Kendrick was making up Anson's mind for him. Tolbert was accepting the inevitable.

Two things happened: Irena was seen in Bluewater no more, except for infrequent visits. When anybody made bold to ask, the reply was, "Oh, she's here and there; Irena has a will of her own." As for Lurie, she had departed for her parents' home and her brother's, and no connection was made. Lurie's love for Anson Winters was, as her sister would note, the best-kept secret on the prairie.

When her sister died, Irena came home and stayed, and people considered her arrival no riddle. After a year, a proper interval of mourning, Anson would marry Irena. But they did not reckon with Tolbert Kendrick. The loss of his daughter had been an unacceptable blow. And then there was the affected child to care for. He had sacrificed one daughter and would not give up another.

And they did not reckon with Anson's mother. Was the affliction visited upon Little Johnnes hereditary? There had been no incident of it among her people in memory, or in Big Jack's family, so far as she could find out. In the Bluewater Cemetery there were two small graves beside that of Tolbert Kendrick's uncle's wife. The dates indicated the mother had not died in childbirth, yet both children had passed away before their second birthday. The doctor who might have attended them was long deceased. Discreet questioning by the cook at Towerhouse, who knew everybody in Bluewater, as well as the skeletons in their closets, turned up nothing.

The Bluewater undertaker was in his earlier fifties and revealed nothing, but it was revealed that his father, from whom he had inherited the mortuary, was still alive, in his nineties, residing with a daughter in Tyler. Bronson was sent as emissary to investigate. Yes, he had sold coffins for all three of the deceased members of the Kendrick family, had dug the graves and helped bury them, as he had for every Bluewater citizen of the day. He remembered the Kendricks and the two afflicted children—two born in sequence.

Thus was the star-crossed marriage to falter despite apparent certainty. Anson's mother and Irena's father were in agreement that the ceremony should never take place, and for different reasons. The father of Melba had sacrificed one daughter and would not risk another. It may be he hadn't an inkling of the Winters family's objection.

Lurie had been away a year and had returned. Nobody save her sister saw a connection. Lurie had an acceptable suitor, a premedical student at the University of Texas, who was her age to the month. She was twenty-six, and by definition of the times, a bit up in years to be unmarried.

Since their marriage, Lurie had never let the names of the two sisters cross her lips in conversation with Anson. The subject was too sore in her heart. She believed that Irena had told him she would never have children, else he would have disregarded all wishes and warnings. Unthinkable. A childless household on the desolate plains of Texas. Yet Anson and Lurie had been married close to three years and had none of their own.

I was their child.

Lurie accounted it significant that Anson never married, or was known to keep female company, until after Irena had married.

While away for a year in Mississippi, Irena had completed a course in bookkeeping, and on returning home, she had taken employment in the circuit clerk's office. Remaining the prettiest and the best-dressed girl in Bluewater, she eventually married the divorced son of the county judge, a lawyer, who sometimes pleaded cases in his father's court. She had been married for four years, and the lack of offspring confirmed to Lurie the correctness of her judgment. Irena intended to remain childless, with the remedy that she had the care of two children from her husband's former marriage.

All of this revelation came to my ears in bits and pieces. Unmentioned were two things that were palpable yet unspoken: Lurie had not given him a child, and in his love life, she was number three.

CHAPTER fifteen

The Flower Pit

HIGH WINDS WERE tearing the clouds to rags. To the south-west, a band of clouds, low-lying and lumpy like the Buckalew Mountains back home, as black as the earth of Chinaberry farm, stretched halfway up the sky and were rendered the darker by the cotton fields below.

It had been a day of both sun and cloud, and the cotton pickers were grateful for any respite from the heat. Occasional streaks of lightning pierced the clouds, too far away for the accompanying thunder to be heard. The pickers, taking advantage of the intermittent shade, ate their dinner hurriedly, skipped the siesta, and returned to the fields.

In mid-afternoon, when rolls of thunder sounding like a wagon over a cobbled road warned of approaching rain, the pickers fled for shelter. They had been in the fields since four that morning. Dark in the minds of all was the tornado that had wiped out a family of four on lands the Bent Y Ranch now leased, some ten miles from Chinaberry.

Anson had shown me the cellar of that family's house one day when we had gone out to check on the windmill. There was the cellar hole but not one remaining plank of house or outbuilding. Anson told me of their deaths in the twister, and I gazed at the cellar, recreating that night of terror and death. He said that a man, woman, and two infants had been snatched from their beds in the night, sucked into the vortex of a whirling wind, flung to their death without a moment to cry out to the Almighty. Seeing that I was now trembling, he picked me up. "Let's go," he said, and carried me back to the truck.

The telephone rang shortly after two o'clock. The operator in Bluewater did not usually take switchboard calls when there was lightning. Wire attracted bolts of electricity, with possibly dire results. But the insistent ringing caused her to risk it. Lurie answered with trepidation. Anson was calling about the weather, and to say he would be coming home early. Knowing about a traumatic experience two years before at my Uncle John's in Alabama, he believed his coming offered reassurance. He had witnessed that the darkening of the daytime sky caused me to tremble.

Angelica and Rosetta were canning pears in the backyard. They had packed the jars and screwed on the lids, and the jars were sitting on a wire rack in the oversized iron wash pot, being cooked and sterilized over a managed fire. With the first roll of thunder, they fled to the Martinez family's storm cellar, leaving their grandfather to tend the fire, wait out the cooking, lift the Mason jars out with tongs, and store them in the smokehouse. Then, as the wind rose, he secured all washtubs, buckets, and pans that might blow away. The storm pit at Chinaberry was between the garden fence and one of the cotton houses, now filled to the rafters. The pit was empty, except for flowerpots stacked on a shelf.

Back home, our storm cellar had been used in winter to keep pots of Wandering Jew and fern below the frost line, and we called it our flower pit. Sweet potatoes and turnips and green tomatoes were also buried there in pine straw.

At age five, I had stood with my mother and sisters at a back window and watched a twister cross our land, doing no harm. A cyclone had crossed Uncle Bob's farm, too, and I recall the fallen timber where it had swept clear a path a hundred yards wide. Every cyclone season brought news of barn roofs lifted, chicken houses blown away, telephone lines down. But the tornado that struck western Chambers County and devastated adjoining West Point, Georgia, was one with more serious consequences.

We had gone there in our Model T Ford to spend a Sunday at my Uncle John's. The home of my Uncle John and Aunt Claude and their eight children was an antebellum structure, two stories high, with lofty ceilings and a porch all the way around, supported in front by square columns. The kitchen and dining room were connected by a roofed-over corridor, thirty yards to the rear.

Shortly after dinner, we had gathered on the porch and were listening to a roar from the southeast, too loud and near to be the Atlanta and West Point train passing. Though the sky had glazed over with clouds, there was no particular threat of rain. Other than the roar, there was an ominous stillness. Not a tree branch stirred.

And suddenly the tornado was upon us. Shingles flew about us like leaves. There was no time to reach the storm pit. Hardly were we inside and the doors fastened than the house lifted and settled back on its foundation, bereft of its top story. The porch was ripped off in front, along with the square pillars, the swing left hanging. I recall that a picture was swinging out from the wall over my head. The kitchen and dining room were intact. In the pitch-blackness of the stormy night that followed, bodies were dug from the ruins of the West Point railroad station.

I studied on this memory very much on this day at Chinaberry when the sky looked similar. But directly after Anson called, the clouds dispersed, the sun came out, and although the horizon remained dark toward the southwest, the cotton pickers returned to the fields. They would remain there until last light, at nine, when you can see cotton and nothing else. Angelica and Rosetta came back to hang out clothes from the wringer to dry. Blunt took the precaution to clear out the plunder in the storm cellar and lay down a groundsheet, and with the help of Angelica and Rosetta, he lugged the half-sized mattress from the screened porch to the pit.

Anson arrived home in bright sunlight, the air cooled by a distant rainfall, perhaps hail. Hail the size of hen eggs was known to fall at times. I met him at the mailbox and was cheered that day by a letter from home. I had now been away from home several weeks, and my homesickness was often sharp and often dull. Mama was saying nothing concerning my protracted stay. She left that to Papa, whose letters to Ernest dwelt on this subject alone.

When Anson arrived, we immediately went for a ride on Blue, whom Blunt already had prepared, always anticipating Anson and knowing what he wanted. We took a trot on Old Blue to the back of the pasture. Lurie went with us, which she didn't always do.

A town girl, Lurie had failed to develop a pleasure in horseback riding, and it was the single activity she did not always agree to when Anson urged her to join him. The ride we took that day, I was to recall later, was the last she had, and the last to which Anson invited her. Lurie rode sidesaddle, by choice rather than by adherence to the custom of the day. At home, on the rare occasions we boys rode in from the field with my father, we sat behind him, holding to his belt for balance. But Anson had settled me in front, a left arm lightly holding me for security.

That day we rode to the backside of the farm, the fields brown and bare from a second picking. We sauntered past a later planting, these fields at their peak of opening, with a white cloud set-

tling to earth and reaching to the dying sky. The sun was setting behind a cloud, and to rural wisdom this meant that bad
weather could be expected. The air was unusually cool, so cool
that the male pickers had put on their shirts. The women, who
were as tan as they were ever to be, and with no fear of freckles,
had unrolled their sleeves.

The pickers glanced up and smiled and did not stop. Their
arms flew from bolls to sack. Blunt was among them, and while
his right hand delivered a boll of cotton to the canvas sack he
dragged along the row, his left was snatching another. Any good
picker worked with both hands, as one might milk a cow, both
hands going like pistons. Blunt always joined his family in the
fields when he could. No one required or asked for this labor
due to his age, but as he considered the cotton farm his high re-
sponsibility, nobody could talk him out of continuing to pick. He
could pick an average of fifty pounds a day, quite a feat.

The pickers did not pause. The children of the Martinez family were paid for harvesting any amount over two hundred
pounds. It was more game than profit. The best among them,
given a daylight-to-dark performance, could top four hundred
pounds in thick cotton. There was a rhythm to the picking, like a
poem rising, verse to verse.

Night came early, for the sky clouded over. There were no
stars. The yellow spot was where the moon was rising. Anson
walked around the house to see that everything was battened
down. The sparrows, heard chirping sleepily under the eaves at
dusk, were quiet. The gloom of the outside came in and hovered
just beyond reach of the reolite lamp. We could hear the flame
burning the kerosene.

To enliven the somberness of the evening, Anson told us
about the latest exploits of the Knuckleheads. He had heard
from Ernest that they had for several weeks been living in a

rented room and were having their meals next door at the De Rossett Hotel dining room, which served all comers with a loaded table. There were no waitresses. The cook replenished any dish that was half-empty. A diner left a quarter by the plate in payment. In the case of regulars, such as the Knuckleheads, payment was left Saturday evening for the week, placed in an envelope the hotel furnished, the name on the cover. Both Cadillac and Rance had left a one-hundred-dollar Confederate bill with a note, "Keep the change."

The upshot was that the female manager of the De Rossett was amused by this. She simply laughed and demanded green money, not gray. She also took the occasion to ask them to tone down their hospitality at the table. Let a stranger sit down, and they would begin to ply him with dishes faster than could be taken until the confused diner was surrounded by piled-up bowls. Insisting on ladling soup for a customer, Rance saw to it that a portion landed in the diner's lap by accident. The apology was always profuse. The Knuckleheads had been known to throw biscuits at each other across the table rather than pass the plate.

Lately they had left behind their usual fistfights and had started something even more childish: food fights. Baked potatoes and chunks of cornbread were their weapons. After one particularly messy food fight, the De Rossett manager had ousted them for good, and the landlady next door had removed their plunder to the porch and locked them out. They now lived in a shack that had been located for them by the manager at the ice plant. The shack was near the Katy Railroad station, and there they lived on pork and beans and sardines. "They're not long in Texas," Ernest had told Anson.

Anson, who had a good head for names and places, told us of the Webb Latin School in Tennessee, where participants in a fight were merely chided. The onlookers were the ones who were punished by lost privileges. Therefore no fights.

Remaining at the supper table long after the dishes were cleared, we sat listening to Anson. Other than his voice, there were no sounds. There was not a breath of air moving. The temperature of the earth and sky had reached equality. The coolness of the afternoon lingered. It was not so much the gloom of the night that oppressed me; it was the remembrances of the moment of terror when I had stood in a room with a picture swinging over my head, when the house lifted, the upper floor and porches ripped away. But maybe it was the homesickness that sometimes gnawed at me, too. Remembering that tornado inevitably made me think of home and my people there. My uneasiness was being gauged by both Anson and Lurie. He said, "Your eyes get bigger at night."

Both Lurie and Anson sat on the bed beside me after I was ready for bed. They couldn't have missed I was trembling. I fought sleep, staying awake as long as I could. Anson liked to talk in the dark before drifting off. It was mentioned that the penned herd on the leased pasture should be soon visited. Blunt would be taken along to grease the windmill and repair it, if required. They would take me along. And this time of year, carnivals and circuses visited town thereabouts, and we would go when one showed up. And Anson had noticed a poster at the Bluewater Bijou showing Harry Carey, who would be starring in a cowboy motion picture this Saturday coming. Anson could abide movie cowboys only to laugh at their novelty. I slept at last, not hearing him intone his usual goodnight: "Sleep good so you'll be happy in the morning. Sleepy sleep. Sleepy sleep."

I waked with a start. I was being carried through the dark down the long hall, onto the screened porch outside, where Anson had to bend to force his way through wind that tore at our nightclothes. Lurie followed, holding to his belt for guidance, two pillows squeezed in an arm.

Inside the flower pit, with the slanting door closed, Anson struck a match to get us oriented. We bedded down on the half bed, my arms around Lurie's neck, my head on her breast, Anson's arms encircling us both. I was secure and felt no fear. I had once heard Anson say, "No mattress is too narrow for two people at peace with each other," and now I knew what he meant, because to be this crowded in such a time felt wonderful.

Morning found me back in my bed, the sun shining, and the pickers were hours in the field already. I jumped out of bed, washed my own face, and put on my clothes and moccasins before it could be done for me. From then on, this was how it was to be.

I don't know why there was such a sudden change in me, but I felt different. I was thirteen years old; I would do for myself. I was not a baby. Both Anson and Lurie stared at me in recognition of my independence, and Anson respected it by day if not entirely by night.

Outside there had been high winds yet little rain. Blunt reported a strip of cotton blown out of the bolls, less than a hundred yards of it. A cyclone had touched down briefly, here and there, and had ripped the roof off one of the cotton storage houses, the one with less than a bale in it. The cotton had blown into the Osage orange row directly in front of it, and where yesterday it was green, it was now white.

"Looks like somebody has some oranges to pick today," Anson observed. "White ones."

CHAPTER sixteen

Questions Answered

A PORTION OF the grassland was rich earth, taken over for grazing as the ranch expanded. Here the grass had been sown and cattle stood knee-deep in acres of clover, and there were even copses of trees that furnished them shade. At noon, many lay as if slain under the water oaks, shifting as the shade shifted, the ground appearing as a wall of flesh, heaving now and then, with a sudden rising at times.

Anson, pointing to a cow standing in a stuck pose in the shelter pasture, asked me, "Do you know what she's thinking about?" I didn't.

"She's got her mind on the baby inside her." And then he asked, "Do you know how come a baby calf is growing inside her? How it got there?"

I shook my head no to the question, but the true answer was yes. After all I was thirteen, had driven cows to the bull on adjoining farms in Alabama, and though short of knowledge about animal obstetrics, I knew that much. I'd never witnessed the actual copulation, being ashamed to be a party to such knowledge and always hiding behind the barn until it was over. Farm boys might be woefully short of insight into human impregnation, but they were privy constantly to the ways of pigs and chickens, and copulation both bovine and equine. Yet there was mystery there, and I had thought and thought about it.

One day I asked, "When cows die do they go to heaven?"

He broke into a laugh and then checked himself. "That's a new one," he admitted. "Never occurred to me whether they did or not. If they do, we've sent a lot of them there."

"Do horses?"

Now Anson, whom I was beginning to think of as Dad-o all the time, was serious. His face was grave. "I hope so," he said. "Why not? I hope my Blue is there when I get there. Or follows me."

"Dogs?"

"That's a question. Do you want them to?"

"I do. I want my dog Jack that I lost to be there."

This exchange of views with Dad-o was naturally related to Lurie within my hearing, with Dad-o adding, "Our boy thinks deep about things. He's got a head on him."

I often questioned Anson about natural things, like why the wind was blowing all the time, at least a slight wafting breeze, when it didn't act like that in Alabama. He had explained to me that it had to do with the differences in the temperature of the air and the ground.

Ernest Roughton, bothered by this phenomenon, claimed it gave him a headache, and he said on several occasions, "Damn that headache wind." But he got used to it, as did we all. There was no other choice.

How would the torrid days of summer be endured without it, though? The moving air became the natural order of things, and what you did notice was that at times it ceased, sometimes inexplicably, and you stopped and tried to make something of it.

Dad-o would say, "Come on, wind. Wake up and get moving."

And pretty soon it would.

So many questions to ask, so many answers to be gained.

Why did ticks enjoy burrowing into one's skin?

I was still undergoing the daily tick hunt. It was the storming of my last citadel, the exposure of my entire body, of which I was so protective, so ashamed, but I had finally relented and had my shirt raised and spied under, my breeches stripped down, and my "little fixings" checked for these bearers of Rocky Mountain fever. Not much was known then by folk generally about this dreaded disease, except that the bite of an infected tick was as dangerous as a sidewinder rattlesnake. Though the Winters family didn't know of anybody firsthand who had suffered from this illness, there were tales aplenty about its high fever, its ravages, its ending in a frightful death.

In examining me for ticks, Lurie now limited herself to my head, running her hand through it, eyeing the scalp. And then, sensing of my neck and shoulders and my heaving chest—I always, at first, would begin to breathe rapidly and almost hyperventilate—she'd stop. "Calm down," Dad-o would say. "We're just a-looking. We're not going to find anything. Just a precaution." And he put a towel, or a cushion, whatever was handy, over my face. When I couldn't see what they were seeing, I relaxed.

There was a single comment made about my body that sticks in my mind. Not once but many times. Passing his hand over my rear end he would say, "That's the softest skin you'll ever feel. Just like a baby's. Press right here," he'd say to Lurie. "Softest little butt you'll ever touch." And Lurie did on several occasions, but mostly she would agree with a "Yes." This was the closest they came to breaking through the invisible protective shield a boy clothes himself in.

So what of bugs? Why did they exist and bother us so?

Dad-o knew a great deal about them, and it was he who put it into my head the philosophical question of how life feeds on death. Which brings to mind a large boy teasing a smaller boy at the Buffalo Wallow School, accusing him of "eating dead chicken." When the smaller one denied it, tears streaming down his cheeks, his tormentor turned the knife in the wound by saying, "Ah, then you eat chicken alive! Run a chicken down and start biting it!"

During his time in college, Dad-o had heard a lot of talk about screwworms and their eradication. And he had to know about Johnson grass, which required drastic measures, and the abomination of chufas—sedge plants that, once they had captured a field, ran like wildfire across it, drinking up the moisture and nutrients in the ground. No known herbicide could stop them.

Chufas were sometimes a plague back home in Alabama. Papa once told us how a man got rich from a cure he guaranteed would solve the problem. In an advertisement in several agricultural journals, the man had guaranteed, money back, that he could rid a man of this herbal pest for only one dollar. Hundreds hurried in their dollars and received the cure: "Move off and leave it."

I also had questions about tumblebugs. In Alabama, we had had these, too. Tumblebugs were hard-shelled bugs that rolled animal dung, or human dung if available, into balls and deposited their eggs therein. The hatching larvae fed on the feces.

In the barn lot, Anson and I observed such a scene, and when I asked why a creature would choose such a manner of existence that was so appalling to mankind, Dad-o answered the question to a satisfaction that obtains to this day. He said that mankind must not impose on other forms of life human way of thinking, social behavior, or morals. Not Dad-o's words in explaining this to me at the time, but they are mine, addressing the same phenomenon.

Life fed on death. I had observed a half-dozen young opossums feeding on the carcass of a dead cow and observed the buzzards so often circling over the pasture. Then there was that troubling wisdom that the Winters cattle were grown to be later killed and eaten by man, as were hogs and chickens, and even the catfish in the lower pond, which had been stocked by hand for that purpose. So man was that much akin to the lower mammals and the insects.

Once, when I sat down to eat, forgetting to wash my hands first, Dad-o said, "I always thought it curious that even a muskrat washes its hands before eating."

CHAPTER *seventeen*

Nino

SUNDAY. QUIET. STILL.

Dad-o had driven away after breakfast. A telephone call had alerted him to meet at mid-morning a representative of a Dallas packinghouse to work out a contract for next year's feeder calves. Those now being finished off were spring-dropped, had been full-fed during the summer in dry lot, and within the month would be trucked to a Katy Railroad siding. They were under contract before birth.

In the absence of Dad-o, as by premonition, Blunt appeared in the yard to watch after me. Lurie called her sister to come spend the day; Velvet's husband had delivered her and departed. From where I stood by the Osage fence, I could hear their voices though not comprehend their words.

Today I didn't peer into the Osage bushes, which were so thick and interwoven a chicken couldn't penetrate them. This I had done several days past, thinking to see what might be nesting or hiding, and had upset Lurie. There I had spied a pair of toy wheels separated by a spindle. Rusty as they were, the wheels spun when I stroked the rims. When I showed them to Lurie, she threw up her hands.

"Where did you find them?" she asked, obviously disturbed.

I told her.

She held them as if they might break. Then, she said, "Don't tell your Dad-o. It will worry him. He wouldn't sleep a wink the whole night."

I assured her I wouldn't. There was no need to tell me this was from a toy belonging to the child Johnnes. I guessed the fate of the wheels. They were handed to Angelica, who opened the parlor door, deposited them, and locked it again.

Walking along the hedge with a rubber ball in my hands, eyes straight ahead, I wondered if I could hide from Blunt. While I couldn't see him, I knew he had me in sight. Dad-o had told me of his and Jack's efforts to outwit Blunt during boyhood. They had never succeeded.

"You can't hide from an Indian," was his statement.

With nothing else to do, I wandered about, planning a ruse and a spot wherein to disappear. My ramblings took me to the barn and beyond. I bounced the ball as I walked along. Going into one empty lot and then another, emerging on open ground beyond, I was close enough to the Martinez compound to hear children's voices, and on arriving at the final fence, I could see the corner of a shed.

The compound was the Winters family's term for the cluster of dwellings, shacks, barns, lots, chicken houses, turkey runs, and cowsheds where the Martinez "tribe" lived, along with visiting kin and seasonal workers.

The fence where I drew up was old and served no present purpose. Some of the cedar posts leaned either left or right. I turned full round, searching about, and did not see Blunt. Then I saw the heads of children peer from around a shelter and disappear. One head reappeared, came into the open, and the child advanced toward me. It was Nino, a boy my size if not my age. He had been pointed out to me once by Lurie, who saw him as a possible playmate. But Nino and all the others who could drag a cotton sack down a row worked every day, daylight to dark. Except Sundays.

Nino came up to the fence and stopped. He said nothing. I said nothing, not knowing what to say. I bounced the ball. We stood facing each other and yet could find no words. I threw the ball over, Nino caught it, and threw it back. We exchanged the ball, back and forth, back and forth.

Presently, Nino turned and ran to the shed and came back with the iron rim of a wagon wheel. He swung it over the fence to me. He returned with another for himself. We rolled them about the empty pasture with our hands until Nino showed me how to maneuver the rims with a short stick held in hand. After a half hour, I was speeding the rims hither and yon.

I felt relief—I don't know why—to be beyond Blunt's gaze. If he could see me now, it would be from a distance, a quarter of a mile. I felt as if a cord tied to me had been broken and I was free at last. It was a trait developed then, and to stay with me, to wish to be unobserved.

Again Nino ran away, to the compound, and returned. He came back with a pocketful of marbles—juggies, agates, cat's-eyes, glasses—and divided them with me. We dug the holes in the dry ground and without a word played roly-hole. The roly-hole marbles game was played in Texas the same as in Alabama. In no time, Nino had won all his marbles back. He divided them again with me, gave first go, and won them back. From the compound I heard the cries of children at play, roosters crowing, the patter-acking of guineas. We played soundlessly without spoken words, fully two hours.

Tiring of marbles, Nino devised another game. From the sheds he brought two poles—center poles used for haystacks. We jumped about like kangaroos. Jumping over a bush, and then a taller one, and a taller one still became a challenge. It was not until I lined my pole up to jump the fence that I was halted. One of the fence posts I hadn't noticed had turned into Blunt. He held up a hand and granted "Yh," his signal for no. But Nino jumped it several times without deterrence.

We heard Velvet's husband drive up and drive away, carrying her back home. And then we heard the purr of Dad-o's motor coming up the lane. Nino dropped his pole and fled home, as if expecting that I would have to return to the big house now that Dad-o had returned.

Not a word had been spoken all afternoon by either of us. And though I had averted my eyes not five minutes watching Nino making his last jumps, Blunt had disappeared. I looked individually at all the nearby fence posts, and none was Blunt.

The next morning, I asked Rosetta if Nino was dumb.

"You mean talk?" she asked, astonished.

I nodded.

"You hear that, Angelica? Little Anson wants to know if Nino can talk, if he's dumb."

Rosetta began to laugh, and Angelica joined her. They made the air resound with their merriment. They clapped their hands and appeared to be choking. Tears ran out of Rosetta's eyes.

When she could speak, Angelica said: "We can't get that boy to shut up."

IT WAS SHORTLY THEREAFTER that Dad-o brought news of the upcoming departure of the Knuckleheads—for Alabama.

I was hurt that they had not come by to tell me themselves, or at least to ask if I wanted to return with them. I suppose by then they felt I was of a different class. I suppose that they, like everyone else in Robertson County, now thought of me as a member of the Winters clan instead of one of my own people back home in Alabama.

I had now been gone from home nearly three months. It seemed like ages.

I pictured the Knuckleheads returning to Chambers County, telling big tales of their adventures in Texas. But when I imagined this, I always saw my own family gathered round, listening.

These thoughts caused a dull pain to throb in my belly, a pain easily ignored, but one there all the same.

CHAPTER *eighteen*

A Particular Day

OCTOBER. The chinaberry leaves were down, and those still clinging to the live oaks were troubled by a chilly southeast wind. Sunlight, pale as winter butter, made stark the brown cotton fields, now picked clean and awaiting a plowing-under. The early September duties that had required Dad-o's presence at the ranch were for the most part fulfilled. The feeder calves were shipped, the roundup accomplished, and the cattle for sale that year dispatched to the Omaha stockyards. What saddle stock they could part with was sold.

The day was Thursday. I was to skip school, which both pleased and puzzled me. Was Dad-o going to Bluewater, or somewhere else, and taking me with him?

This was all the more a mystery as Lurie had admitted to being ill in the night. She was up for breakfast but did not eat. She let Angelica comb and set her hair, an act she usually did for herself. Yet there was no air of gloom indoors. She smiled, if wanly. Her cheeks were puffy, as from a lack of sleep. Dad-o was jovial, and Rosetta chattered unceasingly in the kitchen, more to herself than to anybody else. Blunt had fires going in all three fireplaces of the front rooms.

Lurie saw to it that I was warmly dressed. The jacket lined with rabbit fur recently provided me was brought, and she helped me get my arms into the sleeves. I was to wear for the first time wool mittens she had knitted; a wool cap was pulled down to my ears. I wore my cowboy boots and belt with the brand of the Bent Y Ranch. Everybody seemed to know our destination except me. It turned out to be too delicate a matter for ready explanation.

We went out into the yard, and it was not either the Hudson or the Marmon we climbed into. We would go this day on horseback. Blunt had Camilla, Lurie's mount, for me to ride, and Blue for Dad-o. And for the first time, I was to be helped into the saddle and allowed to ride without any holding lines. Wherever we were going could not be far. At the moment of our leaving, both Lurie and Dad-o grew solemn. Lurie embraced me and I clung to her, in silent commiseration for her illness.

Dad-o and I rode off, not down the lane to the big road. Instead, we headed for the barn and past it, into the lot beyond and almost to the abandoned fence where a cedar post hung in the air. The icy breeze was in our faces. Turning right, passing down the short lane, through a gap, we arrived at a big pasture and still kept going. We were going nowhere in particular. It was to be a day of revelation, with some attempt at a decision.

We drew up at last at a cattle shed, where the weathered boards cut off the wind. Here our mounts stood head to tail, side by side. Dad-o told me that Ernest was under obligation to take me back home within the week. At the mention of home something welled inside of me, something that had been growing. It overwhelmed me.

And when Dad-o asked, "Do you want to go?" I could only nod yes.

He studied me a moment and asked, "Do you want to come back?" And then he explained that Robertson County needed a veterinarian, and there would be no problems about our moving expenses. There would actually be more work than one man could handle.

Did I want to return? I could not reply to this. I was of two minds. I wanted to go and to stay. I wanted to live in Texas forever. And I knew then it was Lurie I could not give up. Until that moment, it had not truly occurred to me.

Dad-o was my security, Lurie, my love.

This was only in part what he had ridden out on that cold day to tell me, while the wind whistled through the loose boards of the cowshed. There was more, and I was left with a mystery. I was to have another bed, to be placed in the room adjoining. Until Lurie was well again, she would need the privacy of their room. I could sleep without being bothered if she was up and down in the night. Dad-o might have expected me to understand, but I did not. I felt pushed aside, abandoned, and in the next moment, liberated. I could have departed for Alabama without looking back.

I was glad, and I was sad, and I could not separate the two.

That night I slept in my new bed in the next room. I was awake both times that Dad-o came in to check on me, to see that I was warm enough, that I was accommodating my changed circumstances. Lurie was up and down all night, and I heard her moving about and Dad-o rising each time she did. I was privy to her retching in the bathroom down the hall. The next day he took her to Bluewater, to a doctor.

The telephone began ringing before breakfast the following morning. If the doctor honored his sworn oath, the practical nurse who assisted him felt no such obligation. The word was out.

Anson Winters was to have an heir.

The Winters watchers had been on short rations for some time. Now they could feast. People who had never set eyes on

Lurie and never would found it a morsel to chew on. Would history repeat itself, with another afflicted child? Dad-o's mother knew this not to be a possibility. The bloodlines were right.

Dad-o—Anson—was both cheerful and grave at the same time. He kept answering the telephone:

"Yes," and

"If it goes well," and

"It's what the doctor says," and

"I'll take either one, boy or girl. Or both. Both would suit us."

Anson's father and mother drove up in the afternoon. Big Jack's comment was, "It's high time."

They had brought the Towerhouse cook with them, and she possessed a caustic tongue. As I hovered in the door frame, I heard her talking to Angelica. "Now Anson won't have to go around picking up other people's young'uns," she said.

THERE WERE TWO more bits of information that Anson would reveal shortly.

Irena and her husband, upon hearing the news of the impending birth, were sending a trunk for the remainder of her sister's furniture and all of Melba's other belongings, which were in the secret parlor room at Chinaberry.

The other thing was that a house would be under way near the Towerhouse as soon as the weather cleared in the spring. Chinaberry would not be home to Anson, Lurie, and their new child. Everything I had known in Texas would be no more. It would, however, stay the same forever in my memory.

Alabama, Alabama

I WAS BACK HOME, on our farm at the Carlisle Place, in Chambers County, Alabama. Returning in the Hudson borrowed from Anson, Ernest and I had crossed the piney scrubland of East Texas, the swamps of Louisiana, the empty cotton fields of Mississippi and Alabama, all in three and a half days. There were no breaking points. The Hudson never once went out to slow us down, as Ernest's Model T had done on our journey west. There were no Knuckleheads to plague us with pranks and insist that we stop in one town and another so they could look about. Ernest drove all day and most of the night, drawing up in a churchyard around midnight for a couple- or three-hour snooze. He slept doubled up in the front seat, and I stretched out in the back, with the wool blanket Lurie had provided for my comfort and a cushion embroidered by her with the longhorn logo of the Bent Y Ranch under my head.

I slept in my clothes, not removing them for the whole trip. I was coming home, dressed as I had gone out, in bib overalls and shoes. The overalls were new; the shoes were fresh from a Bluewater store but not broken in. In a valise provided for me were the undershorts and shirts and wash pants and pajamas Lurie had made. My Stetson hat, the smallest one the company manufactured, was in its box in the trunk, safe from the dust and grime of the road. A hamper beside it held more food than we could eat: chicken fried crisp, sausage in Mason jars, canned peas and peaches and pears, and a box of cornflakes. Ernest had only to buy milk for the cereal and to kindle a fire for coffee. In his wallet, he had a bank draft made out to me, a dollar a day for every one I had spent at Chinaberry. I was being paid for helping Anson to help himself.

Ernest's haste was to meet my father's deadline for my return to Alabama: October 31 at the latest. The deadline had arrived in a letter, and since Ernest's Model T was not up to repeating the journey, Anson had offered us the Hudson. Anson would have accompanied us had it not been for Lurie's condition, he said. Yet he was sending an offer to my father: a house— one of Lurie's rental properties—rent-free until he got on his financial feet in Bluewater; funds advanced, if needed, to move to Texas—a remigration; and assurance of all the business a veterinarian could handle.

Ernest would deliver this mandated offer with little confidence. He knew well why my father had not returned to live in Texas, knew of my mother's promise to a sister who had died from scarlet fever before I was born, a promise to not leave her. She rested in the Rock Springs graveyard, and my mother would never be far away. As for bringing me back if at all possible, this too was wishful thinking.

And Ernest had yet another cause for haste—Ellafronia Cauldwell. Ellafronia had at last broken with her on-again off-again cowboy. Ernest had not been far to seek.

The long road home, the strip of earth balling up before my eyes, had its hypnotic effect. I slept or dozed. Nothing was new now. Crossing the Mississippi, we halted long enough for a tugboat pulling a string of barges to pass beneath us. I looked down the smokestack and felt a hot blast for an instant. The barges were stacked with bales of cotton, four bales high. Ernest waved, and I waved. We were answered by a toot of the steam whistle.

We reached Montgomery at noon on the third day, and we saw the dome of the capitol glittering in the sun. Four hours, by Ernest's calculation, before we would draw up at my house. As we sped up the highway toward Nolasulga, Ecleatic, Wetumpka, and Opelika, the tires began to hum. The song was happening in my head, and the tires on packed earth were accompanying the words:

Brave and pure thy men and women,
Better this than corn and wine,
Make us worthy, God in Heaven,
Of this goodly land of Thine;
Hearts as open as our doorways,
Liberal hands and spirits free,
Alabama, Alabama,
We will aye be true to thee!

We left Opelika, crossed out of Lee County and into Chambers. We left the low-lying range of the Buckelew Mountains behind, sped through Cussetta and Oak Bowery and Boyd's Tank, and then we were in the courthouse square of Lafayette. Here was the courthouse, where Old Puss Irvin had held me up to the fountain as a first-grader, where Joe Barrow always napped on the courtroom steps. Here was the Opera House, where I had seen the movie *The Kaiser, The Beast of Berlin*, in which Huns were busily chopping off the hands of Belgian children. Here was the Bank of Lafayette, which was to close during the Great Depression and wipe out many a small family inheritance. In gathering dust, I could see the statue of the woman of Justice, still holding her scales that weighed men's fate. I had been away; she had not. She was a symbol; I was a fact.

Within fifteen minutes we were parked in our yard, and Mama and Papa and my sisters and brothers were outlined by the reolite lamp in the hall, awaiting us, my younger brother staring at my regalia.

Although I was in new overalls, these were in need of washing after nearly four days of steady wear. I wore my Stetson set jauntily on my head and the wide belt with the longhorns on the buckle, and I stood tall in my cowboy boots, so shiny they glittered in the lamplight.

"He's grown!" my mother exclaimed.

In my high-heeled boots, I stood fully two inches taller. But these were not the first pair of boots with Blunt's scrollwork.

"Taken on weight, too," my father said. "Look at the fat jaws."

I had gained six pounds, by the cotton-weighing steelyards.

"What happened to the freckles?" my eldest sister inquired. "Thought you'd be burned black by the Texas sun, picking cotton."

"We picked one day," Ernest spoke up. "After then we did better."

Papa was surprised. "What I remember most about Texas was the wind, that breeze that wouldn't quit hardly, and if it did quit, you'd look," he said. I recalled but couldn't say what Anson had told me, about the wind.

They looked us over, invited us to the supper table. We were half-expected. There were the familiar plates with the cloverleaf design, the knives and forks and spoons that were not silver, although they were called such.

Later, when my heels and knees and elbows came to notice, these once-rusty parts of my anatomy now as fair of flesh as a baby's cheeks (another Alabama summer would bring them back to their former state), Ernest made the joking explanation, "They kept him in a fishbowl." And then, not to embarrass me, he added, "You wanted him to experience Texas—well, he did, but not what was expected. Learned more in three months than most boys will ever learn."

That evening Aunt Joney, this great wrath of a black woman, came across the fields. She was both feared and admired for her gift of prophecy and her ability to "see through." She called to me from the fence beyond the flower pit.

"Ah," she said on sight. "Something's done happened to you like I said it would. It's writ on your forehead and buried in your eyes. Whatever it was, it'll go with you to the grave. Whoever it was, you'll be looking for them till death takes your breath."

When Ernest presented the bank draft made out to me, Papa looked at it and said, "Huh!" in surprise. That was all. I was rich, and all Papa could say was "Huh!"

Ernest slept at our house for three nights before heading back to Texas. He hung out for a day at the poolroom he had once owned, looked up the livery stable acquaintance, and visited several hours with his daughter, returning with the usual report: "When my son-in-law came in the front door, I went out the back."

Ernest looked up both the Knuckleheads. Cadillac and Rance were back in the cotton mill at Shawmut, feeding spools to looms, and they had many a tale about Texas for any who'd stand still long enough to listen.

They were immobilized for the time being, as the car they owned together had been impounded by the sheriff for speeding. They had claimed their speed was to "blow out the rust," which had not been a good enough defense for the judge.

When Ernest drove away in the Hudson after three days, I followed the vehicle with my eyes as he moved down our lane onto the main road, toward LaFayette, toward Montgomery, the Mississippi River, Chinaberry, the Towerhouse, the Bent Y

Ranch. He drove off toward all those stories I had heard. Toward all those graves. Toward all those people.

The car vanished into the mist of distance, fixed in time and memory.

THAT LAST MORNING at Chinaberry was writ large in my recollection.

As Ernest would be coming early to pick me up, Anson came to my bed at first light with a pan of warm water and a washcloth, a return to a routine now past. I sat up in bed. Presently he sat beside me.

After a while, he arose, withdrawing from me. He went out to the barn and did not return until he had milked three cows, fed the pigs and the rest of the stock. I sat up in bed, but he did not offer to hand my clothes to me, clothes freshly laid out by Lurie, or to put on my shoes. Nothing much was said until after breakfast. There was a telephone call from Ernest, telling Anson he was on the way to pick me up and head for Alabama.

Anson came into the kitchen, where I sat at the table, picking at my food. "I won't have my little salty dog around to prank with," he said. "He's here," he added, with no apparent emotion. But he looked pale and drained.

"I'm not going," I declared.

"They're coming for you," he said.

"I'll come back," I said. "I will."

He made no answer, went to the bedroom, and sat in his chair, the chair we had occupied so often. I stood stunned in the middle of the room. And then we heard the car drive up, and someone from out there called, "Hurry up!"

Anson sat without moving, as calm as the first day I saw him.

From the yard came another call: "We're here! Make it snappy."

At this anguished moment, I sprang toward Anson, fell at his feet, and embraced his knees. He did not respond.

Lurie stepped into the room and said, "Don't go outside."

"I'll not," Anson answered. He watched me grovel at his feet, and when he did not reach for me, I sprang into his lap, crushed his neck with my arms. He held me loosely.

"Get your readies on!" came the call from the porch.

"I'm not going!" I screamed.

"Yes, you are," Ernest hollered. "I'll come get you if I have to."

I pressed tight in Anson's arms, pressed hard with my teeth against his shoulder. The fantasy had vanished. The one thousand miles that would separate us forever were already accomplished.

I heard the hum of the motor in my head.

Anson pried me loose and stood me on my feet, and I caught the frightened look on Lurie's face in the kitchen door. Then she ran forward and embraced me, and withdrew.

Anson looked at me without emotion. "Well, we conquered your rusty ankles, didn't we? Keep working on them."

Ernest was at the door.

Anson turned me around, facing him. "Go home, Jim," he said.

I never saw them again. I grew up; I remembered.

Carol Boggess

JAMES STILL IS A WRITER who leaves his readers wanting more. His works are not long, and in my mind, there are not enough of them. Thanks to Silas House and the support of Still's literary advisers, along with his daughter, Teresa Reynolds, the publication of this special volume of *Chinaberry* is a welcome addition to the Still canon. Not surprisingly, a good part of its appeal is that the story raises more questions than it answers. Still was that kind of man, too. He liked an audience and enjoyed telling stories about his life and place, but it is the seeming contradictions and the parts he left untold that I find most intriguing. My desire to know more about the man and his work has led me to research Still's life, and in the next few pages, I will share some discoveries that may enhance your experience of *Chinaberry*.

Although Still never completed and polished the "Texas manuscript," as it was known, and never submitted the book for publication, he was wholeheartedly committed to it. He had its pages with him in his hospital room the day he died. What stronger evidence could there be that he held this work close to his heart? In giving *Chinaberry* its final form, House successfully accomplished the task set for him: editing the manuscript while remaining true to its creator. Readers who know Still's writings easily realize that the story, characters, and style belong to

Still. For example, we recognize traces of the growing, nameless boy from *River of Earth* and of the troublemakers and the truck driver from "Run for the Elbertas." Familiar Still motifs thread through the narrative: the family under stress, the journey of discovery, the exploration of a simpler time and place, the strong evocation of landscape. The style represents Still's most masterful prose: the first-person narrator who tells his tale in a simple voice, the descriptions of people and places that come alive on the page, and the stories that recreate a world long past. *Chinaberry* recalls the best of James Still, but it is not simply a replay. This piece is different. It is the exploration of a mature writer, a man who was sure enough of himself and his creative powers to move into unknown territory but unsure enough of the results to postpone its completion.

Although *Chinaberry* has much in common with Still's earlier stories, the differences are more likely to interest readers. This boy is not a six-year-old like the child in *River of Earth* but a thirteen-year-old who appears to be six. The setting is not the hills and coalfields of Eastern Kentucky but the ranch lands and cotton fields of central Texas. The prose in *Chinaberry* moves beyond Still's typical understated narrative style to a slightly more self-conscious, sometimes emotional meditation on an atypical experience.

Perhaps the most striking difference between *Chinaberry* and Still's other writing is that this work seems to be told by the author himself about his own childhood experience—a recalled story that explores an event long past but not forgotten. Is this master storyteller transforming his own childhood memories, or is he blending fact and fiction in order to inspire readers to confront the power and vulnerability of adolescence? Whether *Chinaberry* is mostly fact or mostly fiction, the result is indisputable—a beautiful but haunting tale, a simple but complicated situation, an adventure taking a real Alabama boy into a fantasy world in Texas, then sending him back home again, changed forever.

I agree with House that one of the book's greatest assets is the mystery it leaves behind. The following observations do not attempt to solve that mystery or to determine which events in the narrative are true and which are imagined. Instead, these notes trace Still's interest in Texas through his accounts of trips he made there, and they explore his process of drafting the manuscript.

Readers who want to know more about the autobiographical aspects of the story should consult the sketch that Still wrote for the *Contemporary Authors Autobiography Series*.[1] Much of the boy's background is Still's own. For example, Still grew up in a cotton-farming family in Alabama; he was the first son after five daughters; his family had only four books at home, one of which, *The Cyclopedia of Universal Knowledge*, provided his entry to a wider world; and, of most importance, he loved hearing and telling stories, even as a child. Other interesting bits about his teen years that do not appear in the story include the fact that he was twelve when World War I ended; that he played basketball on a local team; that he joined the Boy Scouts and regularly visited the library.

In the autobiographical sketch, he does not mention Texas except to say that when his parents were first married they had homesteaded there and his three oldest sisters were born there (although the 1910 census listed all the children in the Still family as having been born in Alabama). The family moved back to Alabama, according to Still, with the plan of someday returning to Texas, but when his third sister, Nixie, died of scarlet fever in Alabama, his mother would not leave. Perhaps this family history partly explains the source of Still's longtime love affair with

Texas. In Wade Hall's biographical work *James Still: Portrait of an Artist as a Boy in Alabama*, Still comments: "When I was a boy I heard a lot of talk about Texas, and I always thought of Texas as our once and future home. But about the closest I ever came was when I was stationed for a while at San Antonio during the Second World War."[2]

That military experience may have been the closest he came to living there, but he did make an extended trip to Texas when he was twenty. After his sophomore year at Lincoln Memorial University in Tennessee, he stayed at home in Alabama for a year. Late in the summer of 1926, he made a trip to Texas, which he described in a letter to his college friend Dare Redmond. Jimmie (as he signs his letters to "Red") does not state with whom he traveled or the purpose, but he does give a perfunctory account of their two-week journey, including place names and directions, as though he expects Red to follow along on a map. Here is the entire description as written by Still, complete with typos.

Oh, yeah . . . promised I'd tell you about my Texas trip . . . here goes.

Left Fairfax Aug. 31 taking the Dixie Overland Route. Slept a few hours in Meridian, Miss, then went on to Jackson (some burgh). Reached Vicksburgh where we went through the National Military Park. Crossed the Mississippi just as the sun was setting on the water, Tuesday night. Music was playing on the boat and naturally it makes one feel romatic. Its been a long time since I've had another thrill that could equal that. Proceeded to Tullulah, Louisiana where we camped in the fair grounds and slept on a lumber pile. Saw the oil refinery's at Shreveport. Spent Wednesday night near Marshall, Texas. Reached Dallas Thursday, spent the night in a tourist camp at Fort Worth. Went through the Museum and Art gallery there. Saw some friends at Palo Pinto; visited Lovers Retreat (a mirical of nature). From there to Ranger, and saw the famous oil-field; thence to Cisco and to winters where we spent a half day. Spent the night at a tourist camp at Abilene. Went to Anson the next day and spent the week-end with an uncle. I've got some fine cousins too. Real westerners.

Pulled out Monday and went back to Fort Worth. Went South from there to Temple. Spent Tuesday night there. Went to Killeen the next day and visited another uncle. Spent the night a Bruceville. Stayed at a fellows house there and picked a bale of cotton for him in three days. Left Saturday evening and came to Waco. Saw Baylor university. Rode most of the night. Slept at Palestine near a Catholic grave-yard. Spent Monday night in a Mississippi church yard. Reached home Tuesday night about 12.

And that's a that. I will not bother you with detail.[3]

While we now wish that he had bothered to include details, the account does show that he went to Texas as a young man and that the adventures he had there were implanted in his memory, along with the place names Anson and Winters.

Much later, Still made two clear references to this Texas trip. One was in his 1992 interview with Judi Jennings, which is available on the *Heritage* audiotape.[4] The following segment, which is not included in the final edited interview, occurs in the full interview, which I have transcribed. Still is referring to his father having homesteaded in Texas in the 1890s: "Our farm in Texas is now part of Fort Hood, near Killeen. I have many relatives out there, many. But I never went back until, let's see. We went when I was twenty. We visited that farm and relatives or the spot where it had been. And the graves of some relatives are still there at this place. I can see my father pulling up the weeds off the graves." Presuming this is the same trip that he described to Redmond, one of his travel companions was his father. The memory of his father at the cemetery suggests an interesting if vague connection with Anson's visit to the grave of his child.

The second reference to the trip appears in an unpublished piece titled "Was There Ever a Good Poem about Texas?" which was probably written in the early 1990s.[5] Included is this description of the trip he and his brothers made with their father, who was exploring his dream of remigration to Texas:

> Took his three sons along in a Model-T to prospect out a location. It was Depression time. We ran out of money for gasoline. The transmission was acting up. The tires were as slick as pool balls. Papa bribed our way onto the ferry to cross the Trinity River. We ate sardines, slept in lumber mills and in church yards. Papa was a horse-doctor and he medicated enough animals to get us somewhere beyond Waco. Here we picked cotton. The cotton wasn't fully open but we picked anyhow in the unblinking Texas sun hovering at 100 degrees; the headache wind fanning the heat. A cent a pound. We picked two hours before breakfast before the sun found us, after breakfast until twelve. Back in the fields until supper time after supper until you couldn't see cotton. . . . The family's name was Mangram. They lived in a two-room house, a bedroom and a kitchen, and we slept on our cotton sack on the floor. . . . Besides the sun, the torrid breeze which never ceased, our chief complaint was the alkaline water from the well that tasted like horse piss smells.

Though written more than sixty years after the letter to Redmond, this account includes interesting and precise details about the trip, plus phrases and motifs that appear in the manuscript. Recall from *Chinaberry* the cotton pickers' schedule, the "tires as slick as pool balls," "the headache wind," and the boy's biggest problem—"alkaline water."

Biographical evidence suggests that Still's most memorable experience of Texas is this trip, which he made when he was twenty. But he revisited and refashioned that memory many times before he began writing the Texas manuscript, probably in the mid- to late 1980s. We do not have a clear idea of Still's creative process when he was writing most of his fiction in the late 1930s. Several letters from fellow writers imply that he was a perfectionist who tinkered with every sentence, but the copies of manuscripts he chose to preserve do not, for the most part, indicate substantial revision. So the Texas manuscript offers a valuable glimpse into how he went about casting a long piece. As House observes, Still told versions of the story to many of the people he knew well and to some he had just met. Frequently, he would tell and retell the story to the same person, pushing the narrative forward each time. Perhaps he was trying it out on his listeners as he was writing, or perhaps he was simply using them as a sounding board to search his own memory. Regardless of exactly how he was doing it, he was forming the story from creative memory and writing it in pieces. At the same time, he was conducting extensive research.

One of the people he chose to hear the story was also his helper. A visitor from Fort Worth, Texas, Juanita McCulloh was serving as a volunteer with dyslexic children in Kentucky during the summer of 1984. The work brought her to the Hindman Settlement School for a few days. There, at the cafeteria evening meal, she met James Still, whose attraction to her must have been intensified by her Texas address. After returning home, she sent Still a book—*Texas Blackland Heritage*, by Troy C. Crenshaw—that she felt would help prod his memory and "set the exact county." From her letter accompanying the book, we cannot know what section of the story he had told her, but it had made a deep impression: "I can see the man, the horse, and the child, and I can almost hear them speak. It is a story that grips the heart. I hope the material and data are helpful and you will write the beautiful story as you told it to me." Six months later, she wrote him again and included more material about the area that is bisected by the blacklands and prairies. Again, she mentioned the story, this time as "haunting" but also "strong and vivid." Most of all, she remembered his telling of it.[6]

Still's process for creating the Texas manuscript went beyond research and retelling. He left many scraps of paper and full pages that are loosely associated with the project: some in longhand, others typed; some containing large sections of what is now *Chinaberry*, others filled with notes and quotes of interest to him; and still others merely listing words and phrases. Any direct connection between what is written on these pages and the emerging story would be hard to make if he had not marked all the materials with *TX* in the upper left corner. Some bits seem to be offering a psychological context for the story, such as the definition of adolescence—"Period of transition from the dependence and immaturity of childhood to the psychological, physical and social maturity of adulthood . . . from 13 to 21 in boys"—which is followed by these fragments: "his chance to explore life and develop his own values and goals . . . encouraged to be emotionally independent." On one sheet, Still records others' thoughts about memory. For example, in his notes he references Jerzy Kosinski's words: "What we remember lacks the hard edge of fact. . . . The remembered event becomes an incident, a highly compressed dramatic unit that mixes memory and emotion, a structure made to accommodate certain feelings. If it weren't for these structures, art would be too personal for the artist to create, much less for the audience to grasp."[7] Another interesting, even provocative, comment he includes is neither statement nor question: "Could it have happened this way. It was long ago, and I was thirteen, and since have indulged in fiction as a way of life—J. Still."[8]

During the time that Still was working with his ideas and pages for the Texas story, his most trusted correspondent was his friend and fellow writer, Jim Wayne Miller. In 1983, Still attended the summer writing workshop at Yaddo, in Saratoga Springs, New York. Miller was there as well. Although they would have known each other before then, the time they spent together that summer brought them much closer. Still must have been forming the story in his mind, and if so, he would have begun telling it to his friend. Many of Still's personal letters to Miller throughout the last half of the 1980s were signed not James Still or Jim but Anson Winters, or AW, or merely Anson. Was it a private joke, or was Still somehow entering into his own story, not as the boy but as the man, or as the boy grown into the man?

One of Still's letters to Miller conveys an intriguing comment about Katherine Anne Porter, a friend and fellow writer whom Still had come to know personally in 1940, the first time he attended the Yaddo workshop. Miller was writing an article about Porter (whose given name was Callie Russell Porter) in which he had quoted Still's statement that "Porter's version of her childhood was just another one of her inventions." In this letter, Still praises Miller's article but suggests that he reword that statement: "[T]his sounds critical on my part—those six words—I am not at all adverse to Callie Russell Porter changing her name to one that pleased her ears and view of herself, or to her 'inventing' a childhood that never was. The greatest reward for being an artist is that if there is something they want with all their heart and cannot have in reality, they may possess it in fantasy. In Porter's case, this was necessary for her happiness, her relating to her world, in the last analysis, her art."[9] This letter, like most of his to Miller in the 1980s, was signed "Anson." Could it be that a similar sort of fantasy was necessary for James Still's happiness and for his art? Or is it more appropriate to see the Texas project in the context of a quotation of Sholom Aleichem that Still wrote in his notes? "When you die others who think they know you will concoct things about you. . . . Better pick up a pen and write it yourself, for you know yourself best."[10]

The factual context of James Still's Texas manuscript is unresolved and irresolvable, but mystery is a big part of its attraction and force. In the second chapter of *Chinaberry*, Lurie is telling the boy about Anson's background because she wants him to understand and not to fear. The narrator says wisely, "We can never get plumb to the bottom of anybody." That truth applies to James Still, the writer and the man. We will never solve the mystery, but we can hope to experience it fully.

NOTES

1 James Still, essay in *Contemporary Authors: Autobiography Series*, ed. Joyce Nakamura (Detroit: Gale Research, 1993), 17: 231–48.

2 Wade Hall, *James Still: Portrait of an Artist as a Boy in Alabama* (Lexington, KY: King Library Press, 1998), 2.

3 Still to Redmond, 27 September 1926. Courtesy of Alan Redmond. Dare Redmond's letters to James Still are now held at the Lincoln Memorial University library.

4 Judith Jennings, "James Still on his Life and Work," *Heritage* audiocassette (June Appal Recording, 1992).

5 A copy of "Was There Ever a Good Poem about Texas?" was provided by Teresa Reynolds.

6   McCulloh to Still, 31 July 1984 and 21 January 1985 (the letters cited here were provided to me by Teresa Reynolds). Four other letters from Juanita McCulloh to James Still (written between September 1984 and January 1987) are available in the James Still Collection at the University of Kentucky Margaret I. King Library.

7   Jerzy Kosinski, interview in *Writers at Work: The Paris Review Interviews*, Fifth Series, ed. George Plimpton (New York: Viking Press, 1981), 320.

8   A variety of notes and quotations handwritten by James Still were included with the original Texas manuscript. Access to these materials was provided by Teresa Reynolds.

9   Still to Miller, 31 December 1985. Correspondence: box 33, folder 12. James Still Papers. University of Kentucky Margaret I. King Library.

10 The Aleichem quotation was found among the notes included with the Texas manuscript. Access to these materials was provided by Teresa Reynolds.